BOOK TWO

The Brewster Boys
and the
Red Revenge

STEPHEN DITTMER

*Mom and Dad: Thanks for
your love, support, assistance
and encouragement in my
every endeavor.*

CHAPTER ONE

Here we are, the Fourth of July. About a week has passed since our time travel excursion to Pearl Harbor and our encounter with Jackson and Klara. This was the first time we have all hung out together without mentioning anything that happened last week. We can't really say anything anyways since we're hanging with Bobby Newton.

Bobby is a little older than I. He also just finished his freshmen year at Roosevelt High. Unlike Pete and me, he is slightly, well, let's just say that he enjoys eating. Not to say that he's fat, but, he has just got a bigger frame than Pete and I . . . combined. Put it this way, he is the youngest person to have ever won the 'Big Beef Challenge' at Beefy's Steakhouse in the neighboring town of Bransfield. He scarfed down that seventy ounce steak like there was no tomorrow!

Honestly, he is looking more and more in shape every day since he started lifting weights. He had always dreamed about playing pro football but, after being cut from the team freshmen year, I am pretty sure those dreams have been dashed. But, ya never know. He is also the only one of our friends that has had full-fledged sideburns since the eighth grade. I mean these things are legit! Not to mention he drives, which is a big plus in our book! I kinda feel bad though because he frequently plays the role of taxi for us.

He invited us to go out on his fishing boat to view the town fireworks from the lake. It's a fairly small boat, with only one Styrofoam lifesaver and, since it is a manmade community lake, it only has a three horsepower engine. We are a little crammed, but it's pretty cool though, because, surprisingly enough, we are one of the only boats out here.

I thought we would at least see some fishermen taking a break and pausing for the main attraction in the sky. I guess they all had family BBQs to head off to. Besides, the fish would probably be scared away from the boom of the fireworks. Every once in awhile there are a couple of kayakers who paddle by.

So far, our lips were sealed. None of us, not even Pete, have spilled any info about our time travel trip to Pearl Harbor. And, of course, as soon as this comes to mind, Bobby references a fishing trip he and Pete took while visiting Hawaii last year.

"Hawaii! I've never been to Hawaii! What do you mean?" swears, Pete.

"Dude," Bobby retorted, "We went there last summer together! Forget already? We stayed at that pink hotel, rented some mopeds, hiked Diamond

Head and chartered a fishing boat! Whataya mean you've never been there?"

"Oh yeah, ha-ha. I remember now!" Pete says, awkwardly.

"And, if I'm not mistaken, you also took a trip there the year before with your entire family!"

"Oh, yeah, of course I remember. Sorry, man. I'm just, um, I'm just focused on the start of the fireworks, man!" Pete looks over, raises his eyebrows and gives Abby and me a cheesy wink, pointing out his perceived cleverness and ability to cover up his blunder.

Abby looks over at me, smiles and rolls her eyes. Poor, Pete.

"Ha-ha, yeah, man, I love Hawaii, Bobby! Boy, I can't wait to get back there!" Pete says as he nudges my side, followed by another wink.

Bobby just sits there, looking as if he took the whole trip to Hawaii by himself.

"Yeah, uh-huh. I'll be sure to invite you again next time since it was *sooooo* memorable for ya."

"Don't worry, Bobby," Abby says leaning over towards his ear, "This is Pete we're talking about!" Bobby smiles. Pete is oblivious as he skips some corn chips across the moonlit surface of the lake.

The first of many fireworks burst into the humid night sky. We all lean back and look up as they shower directly above us. Pete takes it even further by stretching out his entire body and laying flat on his back.

"Scoot over, man!" Abby scolds while grabbing Pete's foot and shoving it away from her head.

"Okay, okay! Sorry!" Pete says while gently tapping her with his sandal. I swear they like each other. Both of them just need to fess up and admit it.

As we lay here enjoying the fireworks, the opening ceremony of summer, I hear the "Star Spangled Banner" playing on someone's radio on the shore. I can't help but be reminded of the sailors on the USS Arizona and the last time they raised the American flag that morning. It's hard not to think about that day, the people we encountered and how their lives were changed, all in a matter of minutes, all thanks to the Japanese surprise attack.

We, of course, still have the bag of inventions and the blueprint book itself. I have taken complete control over them. I felt it was the right thing to do. I am the oldest and feel responsible since I was the one who got us involved and mixed up in this whole situation in the first place.

We were going to purchase a safe and secure it in the treehouse, but Abby rightfully suggested it would be a bad idea. The logistics of physically getting it up there would be a tremendous task and even if we did somehow manage to get it in the treehouse, safes are pretty heavy. I wouldn't want to see it break through some rotted piece of wood and crash to the ground.

I asked Dad what he thought about me getting a safe for some of my most prized possessions, without telling him exactly what they were. He also pooh-poohed the idea and instead suggested a safe deposit box. He said they are easily accessible if you need anything and are extremely secure. He also mentioned that he had been meaning to help me open my first bank account. So, it all worked out.

So, there the trinkets sit, locked safely and soundly in the Community Bank on Birkshire Lane in the center of town.

Abby and Pete agreed that it would be better for all of us if the items were kept out of sight and out of mind. We would be too prone to taking them out and messing around with them . . . especially Pete.

"*Boom! Boom! Bang!*" sounds the grand finale of fireworks over the lake.

"Oh no! Not again, Jon!" cries Pete as he quickly gets up from his relaxed position and starts rocking the boat.

"Chill out, Pete!" says Bobby. "It's just the last big firing of the fireworks, man! You're gonna throw us all overboard!"

"Oh, oh, yeah I . . . I know. Sorry 'bout that."

Pete regains his cool and leans over to Abby and me and says, "Guys, for a minute there, I thought we were back at Pearl Harbor being bombed again!"

Wow! I guess our whole little adventure

really did traumatize Pete. Sort of, 'shell shock' for the time traveler it seems.

"It's alright, man. It startled me a little bit too," Abby consoles in an obvious white lie.

"Well, good show, good show!" says Bobby as he claps a few times. "You guys wanna head back to my place? I got these cool little fireworks we can set off. They are like, well, these flashy white lights that my family calls *robot strobes*! We walk in front of them and it totally makes us look like we're in a cheesy horror movie, like robots or zombies or something! I wonder if my little bro has already used them all up. What time is it anyway?" Bobby searches his wrist for a watch with no luck.

"Here, I got it," I say as I pull out my phone. "Quarter after ten."

"Cool man, I must have left my watch on the pier."

"No, Bobby," says Pete, "The pier must have left its watch on you! Ha-ha!"

"What, Pete?" Abby questions. "What does that even mean?"

"It means . . . it means shut up, Abby!"

"Whatever!" Abby says with upturned duck lips.

Just as I put my phone back into my pocket I hear my text message tone sound off. I pull my phone out, swipe it open and see a message from my Dad:

-Happy fourth, son! Hope you guys are having fun on the lake! Watch out for sharks!!-

Another message comes through:

-Oh, you got a phone call from 'old man Bailey' today. Says he wants to chat with you soon-

I text back a thank you message and return my phone to my pocket. Wait. 'Old man Bailey?' Who the? Maybe Dad was doing a bit too much celebrating tonight. He should have taken his own punny Independence Day advice: Don't drink a fifth on the fourth or you won't be around to see the sixth! I definitely don't know any 'old man Bailey.' Oh well.

"Ahh, think I'm gonna head home, guys." I say.

"Yeah, me too," says Abby.

"We had a great time Bobby! Gotta love the fourth! All day out here fishing on the boat and then the fireworks! Thanks man!" Pete pounds Bobby a bro fist as Abby starts the tiny trolling motor and begins to hum "The Washington Post March."

We make our way back to shore and dock Bobby's boat alongside a few others already secured for the night. Other spectators including Bobby's family are just beginning their celebrations with their late night cookouts consisting of hot dogs and apple pie. I ask you, who needs anything else?

10

A little girl in a red and white polka dot dress waves an American flag while two boys run by her and twirl their colorful sparklers in the air. All I can think is, God bless America!

"See ya, guys!" Bobby says as he grabs a hot dog right off the grill and jogs over to join his family.

Abby, Pete and I head in the other direction and begin our walk home. I could have taken my bike but it's got a flat and Pete's electric scooter is still charging. That thing is cool, but it's always out of juice. We took it out earlier to buy some fishing tackle from the hardware store but forgot to charge it. It doesn't matter. It's a great summer night for a nice walk back to the oak tree.

"Sorry about that back there, guys."

"It's ok, Pete. Honestly, for a split second, I was startled as well." Abby insists. "Hopefully fireworks are the only explosions we'll ever come across again!"

"Ha, yeah, Abb." I say.

"You gotta admit it though, it was kinda cool."

"Peter!" I chastise, "Kinda cool? We were being bombed and shot at by Japanese planes! Not to mention in a whole different era with no clue how we could or if we *would* ever get home, Jackson and Klara chasing us, holding us hostage, the shootouts, the car chases. Maaaaaybe in a movie, sure, but this was real life, dude and we only get one of those!"

"Yeah and you guys weren't kidnapped,

11

either!" reminds Abby.

"Okay, my fault, you guys are right . . . again."

We all laugh and smile as I pat Pete on the back. I don't think he'll ever fully understand the danger we were in.

Honestly it *was* pretty exciting. Kinda like that one random earthquake we had a few years back. It was totally out of the blue and unexpected and, albeit scary, pretty awesome at the same time. But I can never let Pete know that! One of us has to stay grounded in reality and know that we are not invincible superheroes from our comics.

We continue walking back to our part of town, occasionally hearing a random, stray firework going off here and there. This is the most patriotic I ever remember seeing our town. The gazebo in the park is adorned with red, white and blue tapestries, literally every house has an American flag and some are even on full flag poles and illuminated with flood lights. It's a great sense of patriotism, especially with our recent return from Pearl.

We reach Abby's street, Denmare Lane, and send her off for the evening. Pete and I hop the tall wooden fence in her backyard and stealthily make our way through her neighbor's adjacent property. It's risky since this neighbor is known to think he lives in the Wild West and always has a shotgun at the ready. But it will save us a good half-a-mile of walking. Maybe the reason he has the shotgun ready is because we always use his yard as a cut through!

"Jon, we should just use the time device to travel from now on! We can use it like a teleporter, ya know?"

"Ha, no way, Pete. It's not gonna turn into our own little taxi."

"That's what Bobby is for! Ha-ha," jokes Pete.

"Besides, I don't see his lights on anyways; he is probably out celebrating the fourth! No need to worry this time, bud." I assure.

"Jon," Pete says while rubbing his forehead, "We don't have to worry about, ya know, Jackson and Klara anymore right, man? I mean, I know I was saying it was cool and all, but yeah, it was kinda scary, dude, for real."

"Ha, yeah, bud. I am pretty sure we're safe now. They are still locked up back in the 40's, without their devices. But, more importantly, they are without their blueprint book. They have no way of duplicating the devices ever again."

"That's true, but what about those missing pages, man? What if Klara and Jackson were the ones who took the pages?"

"I dunno, Pete. We just have to pray we'll never see them again, but if we do, we'll be ready for them and give them a taste of their own medicine!"

"We can blast 'em with that freeze ray!" Pete says while making a gun motion with his hand, saying, "*Zaaaaaaaap!*"

13

"Ok, Jon, this is my stop, see ya later, cousin!"

"Okay, man, God Bless America!"

"God Bless America, Jonny boy!" Pete replies as he turns and salutes his prominently displayed American flag then runs inside.

He wasn't joking about the freeze ray. The night we returned, after we took our pizza break and Abby headed home, Pete and I took a look at several other items in the bag. One of them was unmistakably a freeze ray. It had this cobalt blue metal body and was the shape of a gun. But instead of the normal barrel there was a funnel type attachment with a red tip on the end of the entire thing. It kind of looked like a badminton birdie was glued to it. The thing that gave it away was a tiny snowflake etched on the bottom of the handle.

Pete wanted to try it out and I definitely disagreed, so he reached over for it. Of course, knowing Pete, it dropped and the trigger struck a rusty old nail in a plank of wood which activated the ray. It fired a shot towards the ceiling of the tree house and our beloved SR-71 model came crashing to the ground in a frozen mass of ice and plastic shattering into a hundred tiny pieces.

So, yeah, that was the major reason as to why we decided to lock up all the devices in a safe deposit box. Good thing we did, too, before we froze someone to death!

I reach my street, Rickenbacker, and head

towards my backyard where I hear Feeby barking to be let inside.

"Hiya Feebz!" I greet her as she welcomes me home for the night. She jumps up on my leg as I bend down to pet her and readjust her extra floppy left ear. Having enough attention for now, she returns to the back door. As I slide it open, Feeby zooms past me and plops down on the couch. I lie down beside her, and begin to rest my eyes.

CHAPTER TWO

I wake up to the smell of pancakes and crackling bacon on the stove. Feeby jumps off my growling stomach and beats me to the kitchen.

I didn't even make it to my bedroom last night. All that walking around yesterday must have really knocked me out. I push myself off the couch, take a huge stretch-yawn towards the ceiling and make my way to the kitchen.

Feeby takes a few spring loaded vertical leaps into the air towards Dad who is cooking bacon on the stovetop. He removes the last bit of bacon from the frying pan and places it on a paper-towel-covered plate. He spots a burnt piece and chucks it onto the ground for Feeby. "Here Feebz!" he says.

"Hey, Dad." I greet.

"Hey, Jon, hard night last night, huh? I see ya never made it to your room!"

"Ha, yeah I know, Dad. All that walking and swimming and fishing. All day long in the sun, ya know?"

"I hear ya, kid. Want some breakfast?"

"Yeah, definitely, Dad. Thanks." Feeby growls a friendly growl as Dad hands me a plateful of food.

"You may have to rock-paper-scissors Feeby for it, though, ha-ha," Dad says as he throws another piece of bacon on the ground.

"No contest there, Dad. I always beat her. She can only do rock!" I comment as Feeby turns her head sideways as if she knows I'm talking about her.

I walk over to the fridge and take out the orange juice. I notice some of Mom's traditional Fourth of July flag cake is leftover. It has strawberries for the red and blueberries for the blue. I guess Mom didn't have enough blueberries because the star area is pretty small. Most of it is eaten, though, but you can tell the stripes definitely dominate this cake. I will eat a chunk of that later!

I finish pouring my orange juice and take it over to the side table near the bay window that overlooks our front yard. It looks like another great summer day.

I look over toward the Lee's house. Their wonderful flower gardens are in full bloom and all a flutter with a variety of butterflies. The Lees seem to to have an extra boost of patriotism too; an American flag waves in the wind, proudly. It looks like a replica of an older one, though. It only has about half the amount of stars on it as it should. Maybe that's what Mom was going for with her cake, too. The Good ol' Spirit of '76!

17

What should I do today? I don't think I have any dog walking jobs lined up. Maybe I should start mowing lawns with Pete. I wonder if he would let me in on that gig. Hmmm.

"Hey, Jon. Mom told me about some summer history assignment that you haven't started yet for that AP course that you begged and pleaded us to sign you up for."

"Oh, yeah. I know, Dad," I say as I shove another mouthful of pancakes down my throat. "I'll get to it. You know me and history, piece-a-cake!"

"That's my boy! Oh, speaking of cake, did you see there is some of Mom's extra cake in the fridge."

"Sure did, Dad. I'm saving that for later. Thanks! Off to the oak!"

"Okay, Jon. Glad to see you still enjoy that tree house! Be careful. We built it years ago, ya know? I'm not sure we built it to last this long. Let me know if any of the planks are rotting."

"Will do, Dad."

"Oh, also don't forget 'old man Bailey' wants to talk to you. Don't disappoint him Jon. Remember, we can learn a lot from our older neighbors. They can help us relive the good old days from America's past."

Hmmm. Curious. Dad is mentioning that old man again. The same old man he texted me about last night. I have no clue who he is talking about.

"Um, okay, Dad," I say as I pause while

18

walking out the back door. "How do I reach him? Got his number?"

"Reach him? Come on, son, you don't need his number. You pass his house all the time. And isn't he one of Pete's lawn mowing customers?"

"Um, I dunno, which, which um, house?"

"You need some more sleep, kid! The plantation house!"

The plantation house. Okay, this is getting weird. Of course I know the plantation house. I can never forget it. It's where we hid from Jackson and his men, where Pete and I traveled back in time and where Abby was kidnapped.

And now Dad says this Bailey guy lives there. I mean, we know the house and Pete always mows their lawn, but, I don't think any Bailey lives there. Not any 'old man' at least.

"Oh, yeah, that's right, Dad, thanks." I say as I pretend to understand.

Once again confused, I shut the back door and walk towards the rope ladder of the tree house.

"Wallllluuuu!"

Our bird call is screamed into my ear prompting me to jump a mile into the air.

"Whoa! What the heck, man!"

"Hahahaha!"

It's Pete. I must have given him an ample opportunity to sneak up on me while I was thinking about what Dad had said.

"Man, I got you good, Jonny boy!" says Pete

19

with a huge grin, as he slaps me on the back. He must have just finished mowing lawns since he's in his usual white tank top and blue overalls, and is drenched in sweat.

"Dude, you coulda given me a heart attack! The whole point of a bird call is so you don't have to be right in somebody's ear!"

"Ha-ha, you'll live, Jon! I just finished mowing."

"Yeah, I can tell. Done so early?"

"Yup." says Pete as we both begin our climb up the rope ladder into the tree house. "Just a few customers today, so I got them out of the way, ya know?"

"Yeah, I hear you, dude."

We finish our ascent into the treehouse and both plop down on the same bean bag chair, the red one, the good one, without all the duct tape holding it together.

"No way dude, get off." I insist. "Go sit your sweaty self down on the old one," I say as I shove Pete with my shoulder. He pushes himself up with a sigh, gives a hanging German Stuka model a nudge with his head and settles on the blue beanbag chair.

"So, whose house did you mow today?" I ask.

"I don't mow houses, Jon. I mow their lawns! Ha-ha!"

"Yeah, yeah, you know what I mean!" I say as I chuck an empty soda can at him.

20

"Let's see," Pete says while rolling his eyes in an upward, thinking manner. "I got Abby's house actually. Her dad gave me a fat tip too! Umm, I also got the plantation house again and that new family that moved in on Bradenton Avenue. Pretty nice family, with this hot daughter! She's gonna be a senior this year at Roosevelt!"

"Who liv . . ." I try to get a word in.

"Think she'll go out with a freshman, Jon? Man, can you imagine? That would set me up great for the next four years there!"

"Ha, yeah, Pete, but . . ."

"I wouldn't have to worry about anything! I would be the man! Everyone would be like, 'Hey, there goes Pete with his senior cheerleader girlfriend!' I'm not sure if she is a cheerleader, but she sure could be!"

"Peter!"

"Yeah, what man, stop crushing my teenage dream, dude!"

I laugh and reply, "Pete, I'm sure you will have a high school career full of popularity, my friend. But I gotta ask you something about the plantation house."

"Oh, yeah. Man it was weird, dude. It was the first time I mowed it since, well, since . . ."

"Yeah, I know, Pete. Who lives there?"

"You know who lives there, man, the same people who have always lived there, the Spritzer family. They've lived there for years, Jon."

21

"Yeah, that's what I thought. Did you see them today? I mean, today is payday, right? Who paid you today? Ms. Spritzer, like usual?"

"No. No, come to think of it, they didn't pay me today. Actually, I didn't see them at all. That's weird, too, because she is usually there waiting for me with a big glass of lemonade and my cash. Why do you ask, Jon?"

"Well, Dad told me that an 'old man Bailey' wanted to talk to me. And when I asked him where this guy lives, he seemed surprised that I didn't know."

"Let me guess, did he say he lives at the plantation house?" Pete inquires with his brow squished down.

"Yeah, man, and that's the strange part. You and I both know that the Spritzers have lived there for years. Why does Dad think there is some old guy that lives there now?"

"Dude, do you think he's like some zombie-alien body snatcher and he totally took over the plantation house to use as his headquarters to brainwash the whole town, starting with your dad!?"

"Pete, that was definitely the plot to *Attack of the Snatchers,* issue four!"

"Huh? Oh. Oh, yeah! So it's true! Dude! Astro Comics is the only place that sells that series! Jimbo, the comic shop owner, he must be in on this! Quick! Call Abby and tell her to meet us there! Where is the Sherlock 3000!?"

"I'll Sherlock 3000 you! Settle down, bro! What we need to do is go see who this guy is and find out why he wants to talk to me."

"Aw, man, I dunno, Jon. I mean, this is already sounding pretty wild and, well, we just got back from the bombing of Pearl Harbor and I don't know . . . " he says while switching into an elderly person's voice, ". . . if this old body of mine can take it anymore, you young whipper snapper!"

"Ah, I'm sure it's nothing, man. But, who knows? Come on, let's go."

Pete blasts off the beanbag chair with the energy of five ten year olds and begins his descent down the treehouse ladder. I quickly follow his lead and almost step on his hand while reaching for the next rung.

"We can take my scooter. I left it out front," Pete says as he pushes open the back gate and heads to the front yard. I head towards my house, tap on the back kitchen window to get Dad's attention and yell through the glass, "On my way to 'old man Bailey's' house, Dad." He nods and mouths 'okay' as I turn around and meet Pete in the front yard as he starts his electric scooter.

"She all charged up?" I ask.

"Sure is. Hey, man, maybe we should ask Uncle Mitch, I mean, your dad, if we can get the bag from the bank? You never know, that time machine saved us once before and who knows when those items will come in handy?"

23

"No way, Pete. Come on, let's go!"

Pete pushes his foot from the curb and we are off. I am pretty sure we won't have to worry about anything. I mean, Dad seems to think I already know the guy, like, as if the whole town knew him or something. Unless Pete's body snatcher scenario really pans out, then we'll be fine.

We cruise down Rickenbacker and make our way to the community lake. Pete decides to take us off road a bit as we weave in and out the huge boulders that border the lake.

"Pete, your shocks weren't built for this!"

"Ahhh, I am saving up for a new scooter anyways. Let's have a little fun!" he says as he starts humming the main song from *Back to the Future*. "Let's see if she can do 80!"

Pete, the daredevil, gives it full power as we bump all over the place. He takes us over a giant elm tree root, sticking out of the ground. I almost lose my shorts as I fly off the back of the seat. He then zooms us back onto the sidewalk, off the curb and onto the street.

"Whoa! Watch that cat, Pete!"

"Eight lives to go, ha-ha!" Pete jests as the Calico cat hisses at us.

I see the boxwood hedges of the plantation house in the distance as we round the lake. Pete slows down the beaten electric scooter as we approach the main entrance to the plantation yard. We rumble and vibrate down a stony pebble path as Pete steers us towards the house.

They sure did some upgrades to this yard since last I was here or, at least, got a new gardener or something. The hedges are trimmed, the rose bushes are in full bloom and there are no more bare patches of dirt where the grass should be. Guess that makes Pete's job take a little bit longer.

"Dude, they cleaned this place up fast." I say while scoping out the lawn.

"Yeah, man, some more grass grew since last time I mowed it. That's for sure. They better pay me more now. Shoot! Took me an extra twenty minutes to mow this morning."

"I figured it would," I say as we park the scooter, walk around the house and head towards the front door.

The house is draped with red, white and blue banners, in a very patriotic, colonial fashion. We walk up the creaky wooden steps of the porch. The porch itself raps around the entire front of the house. We approach the front door. It's wide and tall with a huge brass knocker, reminiscent of the Jacob Marley knocker in *A Christmas Carol*.

We both turn and look at each other.

"So, what do we say, Jon?"

"Well, I dunno, man. He apparently wants to talk to me, so. I guess we'll let him take the lead."

"I hope he doesn't ask us if we like popsicles and tells us he has a whole case of them down in his cellar, ha-ha!" Pete says, referencing a dubious elderly cartoon character named Herbert. "Okay, here it goes." Pete grabs hold of the knocker and gives it three good bangs on the old, wooden door. We stand here waiting for what seems like hours. We have no clue who this guy is or what he wants. Our anticipation is halted as the door slowly opens with a long '*creeeeeeek*.'

CHAPTER THREE

I feel as if we are in a bad horror movie as the door continues to crack open, seemingly by itself. We hold our breath, waiting to see who is on the other side of the entrance. Our anticipation ceases as a man appears in the shadow of the huge door. He walks towards us and slowly emerges in the sunlight.

"Hello there. Please. Please come in, boys. Come in!"

"Umm, 'old man Ba' . . . I mean . . . Mr. Bailey?" I ask as nervous as I can ever remember being.

"Ha. Yes. Yes. I suppose I am an old man now, quite the old man, actually," he says as we tentatively enter the house.

"Come on, Pete." I say, pushing him forward as he drags his feet in hesitation.

"Yeah, Jon, but who is this guy, really? Where are the Spritzers?" he says under his breath.

"I dunno, Pete. We'll find out, man." I say, reassuring Pete as we walk into the front of the house.

We enter a huge majestic foyer with a grand staircase. I can't believe I've never seen the inside of this place. It's amazing! I don't know if this place is furnished with historically accurate, period pieces and decorations, but wow, is it awesome!

A huge crystal chandelier greets us from above as we continue to walk forward and follow the old man. Its rainbow prisms cascade across the old wooden paneled floor like sprinkles on the top of a chocolate cupcake. An enormous set of stairs outline the entire room as they come together at an upper landing and meet at an arch. Huge oil portraits are placed throughout the foyer as well as antique vases and carved, marble statues.

As we walk towards an entranceway adorned with a frieze of George Washington crossing the Delaware, I notice Pete with his hand outstretched about to grab a nude statue of the Roman goddess, Venus.

"Peter!" I say softly but with authority.

"Ha-ha! Sorry, Jonny boy! I couldn't resist! It's so life like!"

"Life-like? It's made of marble and has no arms!" I insist.

"Come on, boys, have a seat," says the old man as we walk under the frieze and enter a sitting room.

We sit on a hunter-green upholstered, Victorian era couch. At least, I think it's Victorian. I also think I watch too many of those storage auction shows.

The cushions squeak as Pete and I sit down. The old man sits across from us on a more modern recliner.

"You boys want anything to drink?" The man looks at Pete and says, "You must be pretty tired. You did a great job mowing the lawn this morning. You must still be thirsty."

"Uh, yeah, sure I'll take a drink. Whatcha got?" asks Pete.

"How about some iced tea?" says 'old man Bailey' as he reaches over to a side table and begins to pour three glasses of tea. He hands two glasses to Pete and me as he says, "Well boys, I am sure you are wondering what an old man like myself wants to talk to you about."

"Yeah," Pete says while downing a gulp of his tea, "Where are the Spritzers? I gotta get paid, uh . . . sir."

"Ha-ha, yes. Well, you'll find that I have lived here for quite some time, Pete. And, I'm afraid, you may have fond memories of the Spritzers, but I have no clue where they are at all."

The old man gets up, walks over to a ten foot high bookcase and begins to examine his collection, in an apparent search for something.

Pete takes advantage of this opportunity,

leans over and whispers in my ear while keeping his eyes on the old man.

"Jon, we gotta get outta here, man! This guy is crazy! I'm talking loco, man! Insane in the membrane! What the heck does he mean 'I have no clue where they are?' You know the Spritzers have lived here forever, dude. Their house was passed down from generation to generation."

"I know, Pete. I know." I say with a perplexed tone in my voice.

"Well, we gotta bail out, man! He probably hacked them into little pieces! I bet they are buried downstairs in the basement or something or stored in some of these old vases!"

"Settle down, dude," I say while grabbing his shirt tail as he gets up and attempts to head to the door.

"What are you doing, man? Now is our chance!"

"Let's just hear him out, okay? Dad wouldn't have let us come down here if he thought this guy was shady. Just chill, man!"

Pete sits on the couch again and tries to relax. I can see that he is still very uneasy about our rendezvous with the old man, but we have to find out what this is all about.

Mr. Bailey bends down and reaches out for the bottom shelf. He comes back up with two binders, kind of like old photo albums. He brings them over and places them down on the elaborately carved coffee table.

"You alright, Pete?" asks the old man.

"Well, yeah, I mean . . . how do you know my name, anyways?"

"Oh, I know a little bit about you guys. Here," he says as he opens up a binder, "This will explain it all." He turns the first page of the binder and, as I suspected, they are photo albums. The first set of photos reveals some 1920's era images of a man and woman. He continues to turn the pages and a baby is now the focal point of most of the images. He takes a chunk of pages and keeps flipping towards the end of the book. Apparently he is not too concerned with the baby pictures and is looking for something else.

"Can't you just tell us what this is all about instead of flipping through some old photo albums?" asks Pete, impatiently.

"Peter!" I exclaim. "Sorry, sir. Pete is a little impatient, that's all."

"Ha-ha, same old Pete. Always says what's on his mind."

"Who are you, Mr Bailey?" Pete asks with anger and frustration in his voice. And then it hits me: Bailey. In the back of my mind I thought I knew that name from somewhere other than the main character, George, from that old Christmas movie, *It's a Wonderful Life*.

"Hey, that surfer guy looks like . . ." Pete says while staring intently at a photo.

"And . . . and that car! The wagon!" he says.

I look up at the old man, stare into his eyes and say, "Charles Bailey? Junior?" The old man winks and smiles back.

"Jon, that's Chuck! That's Chuck in these photos, man! This guy knew Chuck! He knew Chuck! Or . . . wait."

"It's me, Pete. It's Chuck. Long time, no see, buddy."

We are both astonished. Pete more so, as demonstrated by his jaw, which has since dropped to the floor.

"What the . . .? Are you kidding me? But. But you're old and, and like, Chuck is, well, this Chuck in the photos is, I mean. Oh, man, this is wild man. This is too much!"

Pete was right. This *is* too much. The last time we saw Chuck, he was waving goodbye. He was waving goodbye as the bombs were falling on Pearl Harbor, after his yellow Ford Woody wagon was demolished by a Japanese Zero. He was waving goodbye as the American Pacific Fleet was being decimated and waving goodbye while being worried to death about his father and his whole family. He was waving goodbye to us, seemingly forever. But no. Here he is, older, yet right before our eyes.

"Boys, I know this is all quite shocking to you both and for that, I am sorry," says the old . . . says Chuck.

"Chuck. I mean, Sir. I mean Chuck."

"Chuck is fine, Jon. It's me. I am the same guy you just saw about a week ago back at Pearl, only a little bit older."

"A little older? You're like ancient! What happened, dude?" Pete says as he shakes his head in disbelief.

"Yeah, Chuck. What happened? Why did you? How did you? What . . ." I try to put my thoughts into words.

"Let me explain, fellas. Just sit back and let me explain," says Chuck as he refills our glasses of iced tea.

"First off, don't worry about the Spritzers, Pete. I have no clue who or where they are, but I am sure they are fine. Some things that you have known before you traveled back to 1941, have changed now and for that, I too am sorry. I am sure you have noticed some changes, right? You have been back a week, after all."

"I mean," I say as I take another sip of the tea, "Well, you for one, are the biggest change. I think we knew there may be a few small changes but seeing you was definitely not one of them. Other than that, not really. Just small things, nothing I can really think of off the top of my head besides some changes in landscapes and stuff. I mean the treehouse is still here, our families are all still here, everything like that. I have been sleeping a lot. Time travel sure does take a lot out of you!"

"So, that's all you have noticed? Jon, I

remember how much you love history, you really haven't found anything else?"

"No. Why do you ask, Chuck? Oh no. Did something happen at Pearl? Did something change? Did something happen with WWII?"

"I was going to contact you earlier, as soon as you returned, but I was having second thoughts. Then, finally, I felt like I owed it to you to tell you. And no, the war went just as you said it would. Roosevelt asked and received a declaration of war from Congress the next day and the war ended with the dropping of two atomic bombs: one on Hiroshima and one on Nagasaki. When that happened, everything you had said began to make sense, about the rebuilding of Japan and them becoming our allies and such."

"So what is it, Chuck? Dude, tell us!" Pete says, almost falling off the edge of the couch cushion.

"Yeah, Chuck, if everything went how it was supposed to go, what is it? Oh, man, your father? Was . . . he okay, Chuck? Was your whole family alright?"

Chuck smiles and nods his head. "Yes, Jon. Yes. And thanks for remembering."

"Remembering?" says Pete, "It was a week ago, ha-ha!"

"For you, yes, that's true. But. Yes, Jon. Dad took my advice and left as soon as we did. He told me he had never seen me speak to him in such an earnest manner. He headed home right after that and

34

was with Mom when the attack began. I'll tell you what though; he was very upset that he didn't know where I was. I had to hitch a ride with this guy who was on his way to Sunday service. Dad did feel obligated to head back to headquarters as soon as the second wave was over. I actually went with him to help out and Mom went to help at the hospital. It was chaos, to say the least. But, you guys already knew that then, didn't you, ha-ha."

Chuck was safe. His mom and dad were safe. WWII happened as it was always meant to happen and America was safe. So what could be wrong? What was so important? Why did Chuck track us down, decades later? What does he need to tell us?

"Chuck, I'm glad your family was okay, really I am. But please, what happened? It's great to see you again, although you are more like a great grandfather now instead of a big brother, and it looks like you're doing quite well," I say as I take another look around his extravagant house, "But what happened?"

Chuck reaches down to the coffee table and turns the page of the photo album. The suspense is killing me.

"Well," he says as he gets up and takes a seat in between Pete and me on the couch, "I was hoping to tell you three at the same time. Where is Abby, anyways? How is she doing?"

"She's doing alright. Not sure where she is, though. I could text her." I offer.

35

"No, that's fine. This can't wait any longer," says Chuck.

"I think she had errands to run with her folks," Pete says. "But hey, no offense, uh, Chuck, but how do we know you are really Chuck, Chuck? Like, you could just be some deranged old man who has been creepin' on us three and just be really good with coming up with answers we wanna hear."

"Okay, Pete, I guess that's fair. Go ahead and ask me something. Anything." Chuck says with a smile across his face.

Pete looks to the left and right and then back to Chuck and says, "Okay, what movie did we see together?"

"Oh, you mean the movie I paid for, as well as the food at the concessions if I recall. I believe it was uh . . ."

"Come on, it was only like a week ago!" Pete exclaims.

"Wrong, Pete! It was a week ago for us; it was like over seventy years ago for him, man!" I explain.

"Oh. True. Sorry." Pete says.

"Oh, I know, even though we did not stick around to watch the ending if I recall correctly. It was *Dr. Jeckyl and Mr. Hyde.*"

"Hmmm," Pete says while looking dumbfounded. I just shake my head. Obviously this is Chuck. He knows too much to have taken a few lucky guesses, but Pete is relentless in his Private-I tactics.

"What happened on our way to Diamond Head?"

"You mean when you guys were explaining things to me and Jackson and Klara came up behind us and Jackson had a shootout with the cop and I went over and rescued Abby?"

"Yeah. Yeah that's right," Pete says looking defeated.

"What about . . ."

"Pete, come on, it's obviously him. Enough of this, man. Let him talk!"

"Okay, sorry. I guess it really is you, Chuck. Go ahead man."

Chuck regains his upright, seated posture and begins, once again, to thumb through his album.

CHAPTER FOUR

Chuck turns page after page of his album, telling us the story of his life through old photos. He shows us a ton of pictures of him surfing and riding the wild coast on the North Shore with his friends. The very same friends we met that night at the theatre.

"Hey, there they are!" Pete says, pointing to the guys in one photo, all huddled together in front of Chuck's Woody. "What happened to those guys? How about the 'Doll Dizzy' one? Ha-ha!"

"Oh, Sid, ha-ha. Good ol' Sid."

Chuck pauses as his eyes start to well up.

"I lost touch with most of these guys. It was hard back then. We didn't have cell phones or email or social networking sites to keep in touch when our paths diverged. But Sid . . . I know what happened to him," he says wiping back a tear from his left eye. "Good ol' Sid enlisted the day after we were bombed. He was killed in action in the Pacific. In the last letter I got from him, he told me he was only seconds away from helping the men raise the flag on Mt. Suribachi,

Iwo Jima. You know, that famous photo? He said he had eaten something bad the night before and was stuck in the latrine!! Ha-ha. There was some good news, though. He seemed to hit it off with a nurse who took care of him that night. 'Doll Dizzy' Sid. I haven't thought about him in years. I sure do miss that guy."

Chuck looks up at an old oil lamp on an adjacent table and sits in a trance for a few seconds. He regains himself, looks me in the eyes and then smiles again. I smile back in kind and look down towards the album. Chuck follows my lead and turns the page.

The next few pages, however, do not lead us to more happy thoughts, as I had hoped. They contain photos of the devastation of the surprise attack: a burnt out factory, the naval hospital overflowing with the injured, and an eerie photo of the water, filled with fuel and fire from the sunken and damaged ships.

I reach over and turn the pages, hoping for a more cheerful view of Chuck's history. And there it is: Chuck's first days in college. The photos show Chuck moving into his dorm, his mom and dad helping him unload boxes, meeting his new roommate, and his mom making his new bed.

"Cool, man! Where did you go to college?" asks Pete.

"Well, I went to the University of Chicago." Chuck replies.

"Nice!"

"The University of Chicago? That's where they had some of the Manhattan Project, the plan to build the bomb," I add as I turn the page to reveal more photos of Chuck in college, playing basketball, rushing for a frat and then, passed out on the frat couch.

"Yup, sure is. Turn the page one more time, Jon. I'm sure you'll enjoy it."

I turn the page once again to reveal . . . photos of the Manhattan Project!

"Chuck! Is this?"

"Yes it is. I know you boys probably thought I was just a simple surfer, but I excelled in science and actually majored in physics. I was extremely lucky to be one of the few students to observe Enrico Fermi and his team conduct the first controlled nuclear reaction at the University of Chicago."

"No way!" says Pete.

"Yeah, didn't this take place under a tennis court or something?" I ask.

"Yes, a squash court actually, ha-ha."

"Chuck, these photos are priceless!" I say.

"Yeah, man," Pete chimes in, "You could get so much money for these! Take them to that famous pawn shop in Vegas!"

"Ha, no, no I could never do that, fellas," says Chuck as he cracks a smile.

"How were you able to get in on this, Chuck? I mean, you were just in Hawaii and all of a sudden you have front row seats to the Manhattan Project? Next thing ya know you'll tell us you were there to watch the dropping of the Gadget in Los Alamos!"

"Well, Jon . . ."

"Wait. What!? Are you kidding me?"

"Well, we can leave that story for another day, my friend."

"So how, Chuck?" asks Pete while finishing off his iced tea.

"Well, I majored in physics and my professor was an old school buddy of my father's. He ensured that I got to see, and, actually take part in that monumental event. But even though I was privy to something as top secret as the atomic bomb, I was preoccupied with the temporal device. It's all I thought about," he explains.

"I began to minor in theoretical physics and quantum mechanics. I did my best, throughout my college career and after, to not only duplicate the time device, but to perfect it."

"But how would you even begin to know . . . Chuck, no way. Did you . . . were you the one who ripped out those pages from Von Wexler's blueprint book?" I pause and wait for a response. Chuck's face droops like a wrinkly puppy.

"I'm sorry, Jon, really I am. Believe me you don't know how sorry I am; that decision caused all of this to happen."

"Dude, no way! I defended you! I can't believe Abby was right!" I proclaim as I smack

41

myself on the forehead.

"Hold up, Jon, let's hear him out," says Pete, hoping for the best in Chuck.

"I didn't do it out of malice, Jon; I just wanted to protect my family, to protect America. I wanted to pick up where you guys left off, to prevent any other Klara and Jackson from screwing up history. But, alas, the road to hell is paved with good intentions. My whole plan backfired on me."

"What happened, Chuck? You still haven't told us what happened. What went so wrong? What's wrong with the present?" I ask.

Chuck exhales and turns the photo album page once again. He takes his index finger at the top of the page and drags it down to the last photo. The photo shows Chuck, slightly older than in the previous pictures. He is standing with another guy. They are both dressed in lab coats.

"Who is that, Chuck?" asks Pete as he squints to get a closer look.

"That's Oliver Palmer. He was my roommate in Chicago for three years and my lab partner, too. We were the closest of friends."

"He looks like an okay guy, but . . ." says Pete.

I finish his thought with, "But, I'll bet he is the new Jackson, isn't he, Chuck?"

Chuck lets out a very tired sigh and responds, "I'm afraid so, Jon. To a degree, I'm afraid so."

He puts his hand on his head and begins to shake it from side to side.

"I hadn't even done a preliminary schematic on my version of the temporal device, hardly got out all the bugs and he stole it from me: my device, my schematics and the original pages torn from the blueprint book. I doubt he even knew what it was until he got his hands on it. It's not that he wasn't a top rate student, but he always liked to snoop on his competition, to use their research to one up them with it, with a minor, usually, useless addition."

"But wait, Chuck. We have the blueprint book at home and the blueprints for the primary and secondary device are still in it, not to mention, in German." I declare.

"That's true, but the back of the book had the final versions. If you look through the whole book you will find there are many different schematics of the temporal. And as for German, I used to date a German linguistics major. Believe me it was hard to throw out certain words to get her to translate without telling her what I was doing. But, with a little persistence and also help from a German-to-English dictionary, I made it through the specifications."

"Gotcha." I say. "Okay, so continue."

"Well, we had a falling out during our junior year. He thought that America was taking too much credit for the victories over the Nazis when the Soviet Union had been battling them since June of '41, due to Operation Barbarossa. He said that we should have opened up a new front long ago, way before Operation Overlord. You boys know what that was, right?"

"The beaches of Normandy: D-Day," Pete says.

"That's right, Pete. Oliver kept complaining over and over that Roosevelt, the secretaries of Navy and War and the rest of the government had no clue what the hell they were doing. And all the while, the Russians were dying on the battlefield in tremendous numbers and we were safe and sound in the states. And, to a degree, I guess he had a point. I recently read that by the end of the war, military and civilian casualties in the USSR were almost 25 million. That's more than all the other combatants combined."

"Well, that wouldn't have had happened if it wasn't for Stalin constantly purging his own military leaders all the time!" I add.

"I know that's true, and you and Pete know that's true, but he didn't think so," says Chuck. "It is true that the Russians were undersupplied and under skilled and the majority of their defense was to rely on their scorched earth policy. But, I believed and still do believe we did what was right. America, the Brits and the French had to have proper planning or else D-Day would have failed and the war in the Atlantic would have raged on."

"So that's what did it? That's what broke you two up? You were the best of friends and your view of the US strategy was different than his, so he left and got revenge by stealing your work?"

"Yeah, friendships have broken up over less, ya know? Oh yeah, I forgot to mention . . . he was Russian."

CHAPTER FIVE

This is crazy. All of it. We are only back to the present for a week and Chuck, now in his eighties or nineties, I don't dare ask, is telling us about a new situation. A situation that arose only because he *thought* it would help us out in the future. And now, now he tells us that a Russian was helping the US work on the Manhattan project?

"Whoa! What! A Russian?" asks Pete as he turns and looks at me. "But I thought you said his name was um, Oliver or something? That doesn't sound too Russian to me, huh, Jon?"

"Well, his real name is Vasily Mishnev." Chuck continues to explain. "While in the states, he used a pseudonym to try to blend in with the rest of us college kids. He was one of the most brilliant young minds of the Soviet Union. We had a deal with the Kremlin that would let him assist in our attempt to build the first atomic bomb. We didn't tell them what we were working on, however, and boy did we keep an eye on him."

46

"I'll say! He could have given top secret info to the Soviets, right before the start of the Cold War!" I announce.

"That's true and that's why they made him room with me. I was to hang out with him and stay with him twenty-four seven. Funny though, with Klaus Fuchs, The Rosenburgs, and others, the Russians still stole our secret atomic info. They didn't need Vasily for that. He was just a distraction, a decoy. We were so worried about keeping an eye on him that we allowed other, *real*, Soviet spies to infiltrate our program."

"I bet he hated that, being used as a simple distraction?" Pete says.

"It was actually his idea. He knew there would be way too much coverage on him, so it was the perfect plan for the Soviets to employ other spies."

"Okay, so, I hate to put it this way, Chuck, but, can you just tell us what happened? If he didn't steal plans from the Manhattan Project, what in the world did he do? Not that that would matter, because, I hate to tell you, but that happened in our reality too, well before we went back and met you at Pearl."

"Fair enough, Jon. I tend to beat around the bush in my older years. Boy it's so nice to see you guys again. I wish we had more time to hang out when we, well, when *I* was younger."

"Alright, fellas," he continues, "long story short, I know, I know, too late. Ha-ha. Long story

47

short, Vasily ended up wanting to defect. He came to his senses and saw that he'd have a better life in the states, rather than his miserable life in Communist Russia. He pled for political asylum. But once the American government found out he was the decoy to the real spies in the Manhattan project, they wouldn't allow it. He was upset or as you would say, pissed."

"He went back to the USSR and never revealed that he attempted to defect. He turned his temporary love of America back into hatred and grew an extreme sense of Russian nationalism."

"Chuck, what did he do??!!"

"It's coming, Jon. It's coming. He continued his life in Russia and rededicated his life to the Soviets. He got in good with the Politburo, the policy makers in Soviet Russia," Chucks says while looking at a very confused Pete. "In the late 50's he became Khrushchev's right hand man."

"To my knowledge, he didn't work on perfecting the temporal device until after the Cuban Missile Crisis. Once he found out that the Americans made an 'under the table' deal with the Soviets which made them look like they were the ones backing down, he felt he had to fix things. Fix things the way he thought they should have been for Russia."

"Chuck!"

"Okay. Okay. He built the machine, perfected it, went back in time and made it so the Russians made off as the winner of the Cuban Missile Crisis. Jon, the Cold War never ended. Vasily went back in time and warned Krucshev that Russia ended up looking like the loser. Specifically, he went back in time to the 50's, met with his earlier self, told him to get started on the time machine and told Khrushchev to do things differently. Khrushchev did things differently alright. Russia made the same moves during the Cuban Missile Crisis, but used it as yet another distraction and deployed a full scale amphibious invasion from the west."

"WHAT!" I ask in disbelief.

"I'm sorry, boys. I'm afraid it's not the America you know anymore. It's quite smaller now. I'm so sorry." Chuck begins to sob and cry.

"It's okay, Chuck, believe me. We also made a ton of blunders when we went back." I say, trying to make him feel better.

"Jon, none of our blunders got America invaded by the Soviet Union!"

"Peter!"

"No, no. It's true, Jon," says Chuck. "Pete's right."

Things were starting to make sense. Some things had changed. Minor changes, but changes nonetheless. The crazy dog that always used to chase us, all of the US flags with less stars on them, Mom's cake, and of course, Chuck living in the plantation house. Damn! Had I only gotten started on my summer assignment earlier, I bet I would have realized that something went wrong.

"Chuck, do you have a current map?"

"Yes, I was going to show you that next," Chuck says as he reaches under the coffee table and pulls out a World Atlas. He pushes the photo album aside and thumbs through the index of the atlas. He finds the page number, turns the page and spreads the book open.

I can't believe it. I just cannot believe this. Here I thought we were safe and sound and everything was back to normal. We thought our biggest fear was if Klara and Jackson would somehow find their way back to us. But this is crazy!

The map reveals the United States, but Chuck was right; it wasn't a depiction of *my* United States, of the 'Nifty Fifty' that we all know and love. The USSR now had control of more than half of the states. It looks like they used the Mississippi River as their boundary line.

"Whoa, this is heavy, man! What happened to Texas?" Peter asks while pointing at the map. The majority of Texas was still intact, albeit still surrounded by the USSR to the North, West and East. The only part that looked to be under the control of the Soviet Union is a little portion of the panhandle.

"Yeah, the Texans fought back with all their might. When they got cut off from the US Army, they had to take care of themselves. And take care they did. They were able to push the Soviets back, and regained almost 100% of the original Texan territory." Chuck explains.

"Don't mess with Texas! Right, Jon! Ha-ha!"

Pete says as the room goes quiet and a cricket chirps in the next room. "Oh . . . sorry, just tryin' to lighten things up a bit!"

"Chuck," I ask, "If you just went on living your life like normal and never got to build your own temporal device, how did you know that Vasily was behind all of this?"

"I hadn't seen or heard from him in decades. That was until I got a phone call in the early 80's. I don't know how he tracked me down, probably an old spy friend I guess. He was on his death bed. He passed just hours after he called me. He told me the story and apologized up and down and begged forgiveness. I believed him immediately because I knew you guys would have mentioned such a huge event like this when you were back in Oahu. His dying wish was for me to help him undo what he had done. And of course, with your experience, you were the first people I thought of. I need your help, boys. You need to go back and set things right."

Pete stands up, exhales and puts his hands on his hips. In his best Arnold impression he says, "We accept the mission. We will travel back in time again and set things right. Now everybody, get to the choppa!"

"Ha-ha," laughs Chuck. "I finally get one of your movie references, Pete!"

Chuck, Pete and I continue to discuss details. We learn all the important information we need to know in order to, well, hopefully set things right. We did it once before. I hope we can do it again. I thought for sure that we would have to deal with time travel once again; I just didn't expect it to be so soon.

Chuck walks us to the front door and says one final farewell.

"Okay, fellas, if all goes well, this will be the last time I see you." Chuck says.

"What do you mean, Chuck?" asks Pete.

"Well, if nothing ever happens and everything is set right, the way it should have been, the way you two are accustomed to, then I wouldn't have had to track you down and move into this old house. Everything would go back to normal. The United States would be back, the Cuban Missile Crisis would have happened the way it happened and your neighbors, the Spritzers, would still live in this old plantation house."

"Oh, wow, okay. I get it now, I think." Pete says with a dubious intonation.

"Yes, sir. And no one will know that any of this ever happened, just the way it should have been in the first place, had I not taken those blueprint pages."

"It's okay, Chuck," I say while patting him on his back. "But, hey, you don't have to visit us in the future just to give us bad news! You can visit us anyways, ya know?"

"Ha, ha. Okay, well, I hope my past self gets that message, Jon," Chuck says as he closes the door.

CHAPTER SIX

We arrive back at the oak and climb the rope ladder to our treehouse. The walk home was a blur. We didn't say a word to each other. If we did, I don't remember it. All I remember is what Chuck told us.

We lie here, each on our own bean bag chair, staring up at the ceiling of the treehouse, watching the model planes as they sway to and fro in the occasional gust of July wind.

"So what do we do, Jon?"

"I dunno, Pete. I just don't know. I know we can't just sit here and do nothing but, I have no clue how we should attack this, man."

Pete nods his head and sits up straight.

"Yeah, but we gotta do something, and fast. Who knows what else could happen the longer we wait!"

He's right, of course. I know he's right and he knows he's right. But it's so much easier to just lie here and pretend like everything is okay. Of course, I know we have to do something. We are, after all, in part responsible for the whole thing.

"Okay, Pete, here's what we'll do."

"Walllluuuu. Walllluuuu," cries our bird call from under the treehouse.

"It's Abby!" yells Pete as he gets up and heads toward the entrance. He lifts up the hatch and sticks his head out. He looks left and right and left again.

"Abby?" He pushes himself back up and lets gravity close the hatch.

"She comin' up?" I ask.

"Naw man, I didn't see her. I guess it was the real thing maybe?"

"The real thing? Come on, Pete, our bird call is indigenous to the Hawaiian Islands. You know that!"

"Oh. Oh, yeah!"

Poor Pete. I swear, one minute he is brilliant and full of common sense but the next minute he is a space cadet off in LaLa land!

He opens the hatch and looks out once again.

"Whoa!!!" he says grabbing his chest as Abby peeks her head into the treehouse.

"Fooled ya! Ha Ha Ha!" Abby says as she finishes climbing in.

"You almost killed me, Abby!" Pete says while still clutching his chest.

"Oh please. You'll survive! What've you guys been up to all day? Me, well I just got done getting a hat trick in a pick-up game down at the park. You guys should really join me sometime. I know you don't dig soccer as much as I do, but you'd have a great time. Everyone was there: Jack, Ellis, Kyle, Jake, Jeremy, Claudio, Jonathan, Keni, . . . I mean everyone!"

"Abby, we have to tell you something." I tell her.

"What is it, Jon? Did you guys get back at me and pick up your weeklies before me this time?"

"No, Abby, it isn't about comic books. Take a look at this." I walk over to the corner of the treehouse and shuffle my foot through some of the junk on the floor: a radio controlled car that is missing its remote, an old slinky and yet another empty bag of potato chips. I finally clear enough debris to find my history book, the history book that I am supposed to use to do my summer assignment for AP history.

I bring it over and plop it down on the floor. "Brace yourself, Abby. You're about to get a rude awakening," I tell her as I thumb to the back of the book searching for the atlas section. I reach a map of North America and the current United States. Abby leans over and looks down at the book.

"Yeah? So? It's a map of the US and Canada. Sorry, Jon, but I'm not blown away. I've been looking at maps since grade school. Are you sure your class is advanced placement?"

"Look closer, Einstein! Look at the key." I say to my sassy little friend. Abby gives me her infamous duck lips and looks back at the map with a

55

focus on the color-coded key. It takes a second, but it finally clicks in. She starts reading it to herself but finishes the contents of the legend aloud.

"What the . . .? Okay, good joke, guys. Ha-ha. Reeeaaal funny. I got news for ya, April Fool's day is a long way off. Gotta hand it to you though, this book looks quite legit . . .Okay, why aren't you guys laughing? Oh jeez, this is real isn't it? But, but, how? It can't be! It says here that the red section of the map is the North American territory of the Soviet Union? And that the Blue section is the USA. But, Jon, the blue section is hardly half of the USA? What's goin'on?"

"Long story, Abby," says Pete, "Chuck *was* the one who took the missing blueprints."

"I knew it!" says Abby.

"Just listen!" Pete scolds. "He took them, they got stolen, another machine was made, his roommate convinced the USSR to go hardcore on the US and, for some reason, this time it worked. The West Coast, the Mid West, the Pacific Northwest, all of it is gone. It's all theirs now." He finishes and glances at me. I nod in approval.

"Well, we have to fix it right, guys? I mean, we are going to fix it? My grandparents live out in California, or, at least they did. Oh, man, I hope they are okay. Is there like a Berlin Wall in American now or what, guys?"

Abby frantically thumbs through more pages of the book and, as if we were all meant to see it, lands right on a two page spread of the Soviet takeover.

"You were close, Abby," I say as I look at the caption of one photograph:

The Mississippi Wall was erected in 1963.

"That's just two years after the Soviets put up the Berlin wall in 1961, dividing Communist East Berlin from Democratic West Berlin." This gets more intense as we continue to scan through the photos and read on.

"MESSAGE RECEIVED," announces Pete's phone. Pete takes his phone, swipes his unlock code and reads his message.

"What's it say, Pete?" asks Abby.

"Man," Pete says as he lets out a big sigh, "This is crazy. I texted my mom about my aunt and uncle. Ya know, her sister and brother-in-law. I asked how they were doing. Look." Pete holds the phone towards Abby and I."

The message reads:

-Aww, sweetie, they are still in the Arizona work camp. You know that ☹-

Okay, now I don't even want to know what this alternate timeline has done to *my* grandparents!

"What's the plan?" Abby insists.

"Well," I say, scratching my head, "I guess we're gonna need to get the bag from the bank."

"The whole bag?" asks Pete.

"Yeah, man. Not just the temporal device. Who knows what other items may come in handy."

"But, Jon," Pete says in a game show announcer voice, "We don't even know what half of them do!"

"He's right," Abby agrees. "And we don't have time to test them out. We should only take what we need and leave the rest there."

"I guess you're right, but I *am* taking the freeze ray." I say.

"Agreed!" Abby says.

"Alright, I'll get Dad to take me to the bank tomorrow to help open the safe deposit box. Man is he gonna be pissed!"

"Ha, yeah, dude," says Pete, "We just opened that thing."

"Well, yeah, but we had no idea we would need the stuff so soon."

"True."

"So, we're just gonna go back to when Chuck took the plans from us?" asks Pete.

"No, no. We don't want to create anymore interference with the time and space that we already went back to. Can you imagine running into ourselves back at Pearl, the state we were in?

I'll tell you one thing, I'd be pissed at myself, knowing that we somehow made a blunder and had to go back already."

"Yeah, we would automatically start blaming you, Pete, ha-ha!" Abby playfully jests as she nudges Pete in the belly.

"Very funny! But, yeah, that's probably true. So, where and when are we going then, Jon?"

"Well," I say as I pause to think of the best answer. "I guess we should go take it from Chuck, himself. Ya know? Maybe sneak into his college dorm, kinda just like the Russian guy did. Only we'll have to do it first."

"Yeah, that makes sense. Everything was fine until Vlad the Impaler got a hold of it!"

"Okay, well that's one thing we have to ask Chuck tomorrow, then. I mean, the now Chuck, the older, gentler, Chuck," says Abby, politely.

"The coordinates. Yeah we'll need to know them and also the date and location of his dorm." I agree.

"Alright," says Pete, "So, I mean, it should be pretty easy right? Just go back in time, find the device, 'cuz it always seems to get lost when people use it, and break into Chuck's dorm on the campus of the University of Chicago. The very same campus where the Manhattan Project is taking place. Yeah, there won't be any added security, nothing like that to worry about at all. Not to mention, our clothes. Did you guys forget about that again?"

"Chill out Pete," says Abby. "The Manhanntan Project was top secret for a reason. There is no way regular 'run of the mill' students knew anything about it even though it was going on right under their feet. So we don't have to worry about that at all. The clothes thing is kind of an issue, though, I guess. We'll stick out like sore thumbs if we go back wearing what we're wearing now." Abby confirms.

"Okay, add that to the list. Well, we can stop at the thrift store in town. I guess spending a few dollars on some old clothes is worth giving America back its freedom."

"Damn, skippy!" says Pete with a Southern drawl, followed up with a, "'Merica!"

"Alright. Abby, can you take care of that for us, while Pete and I get the device from the bank?"

"Sure, Jon. Yeah, I'll get a nice dress and some heels for you Pete!"

"HaHaHa!" I laugh a huge laugh,"Got'em!"

We continue to discuss our plans in the treehouse. Our plans to, I can't believe I am saying this, go back in time . . . again.

We talk all night, trying to work things out. We set our meeting place at the plantation house and plan to leave at noon. There we can say farewell to Chuck and see if he has any other useful information for us. We also agree to tell our folks that we're going on another fishing trip with Bobby Newton. At least that will give us all day to be gone, kinda cover our tracks a bit.

We finish our discussion, say our farewells and exit the treehouse.

CHAPTER SEVEN

"Arf, Arf!" says Feebz, greeting me as I enter the back door.

"Hey girl," I say as I bend down and give her a pat on the head. Her tail wags back and forth with glee as she shuts her eyes while I pet her and rub her ears. She enjoys it so much that her back right leg begins to repeatedly slap the floor.

I walk through the back room and head towards the kitchen where Mom and Dad are eating dinner at the table.

"Hey, son. We called you for dinner but I guess you guys didn't hear us."

"It's okay Dad, thanks, I'll eat now. Is there anymore left?" It doesn't surprise me that we didn't hear Dad calling for us. We were all so entranced with our plans to save America.

"Sure, Jonny," Mom says, "Let me fix you some," she says as she pushes her chair back to get up.

"No, no, Mom. That's okay. I got it." I say as I head to the stovetop.

On top of the oven is an amazing looking, freshly baked lasagna. I cut into it, grab a huge slab, toss it in a dish and head back to the dining room table. On my way to the table I see a newspaper on the kitchen counter.

It reads:

"Upcoming Anniversary of Soviet Takeover God Save Our Friends in The West."

Seeing that headline kind of kills my appetite, but I pull out a chair and sit down anyway. I dig in and take a couple of bites. It's delicious as always.

"Guys, what do you remember about the, the takeover, ya know?"

They both sit quietly as I shove another mouthful of lasagna down my throat. I look at them both and feel as though I just talked about the elephant in the room. Mom pushes her chair away from the table and exits.

Dad clears his throat and says, "Son, you know she doesn't like to talk about that."

"Huh?"

"Well, you know she has a lot of family in the Midwest, actually, all of her family is out there. I know she never talks about them much. That's just because it gets her so down."

"Oh, yeah? You mean kinda like how she doesn't like to bring up when her brother was shot down in the Middle East?"

"The Middle East? What are you talking about, Jon?"

I swallow my current mouthful of lasagna and say, "You know, he was in the air force and was shot down over …

"Bradley was never in the air force, Jon. He . . . he was never in anything. He died in a work camp in the 80's with the rest of your mother's siblings."

"Oh, man. Dad, I'm, I'm sorry. I . . . I had no idea."

"Well, you should have had some idea, I mean. You feeling alright, Jon? First you sound like you have no clue who 'old man Bailey' is, then you don't remember what happened to your Uncle Bradley," he says as he reaches over and feels my forehead.

"No, I'm fine, Dad. I, just . . . sorry my mind isn't here right now. I should go apologize to Mom.

"It's okay, Jonny," Mom says as she comes up behind me and puts her hand on my shoulder.

"What did you want to know?" She sits down at her chair.

"Oh, Mom, I'm so sorry. I don't know how that slipped my mind. I mean, I was just up in the oak, looking at my summer assignment and I-"

"It's about time you'd had!" Dad says.

"Ha, yes sir." I agree.

"Go, on." Mom says.

"Well, I was reading about the takeover and well, I always learn better hearing it firsthand. I know you guys may not remember too much since you were so young but, could you just give me a rundown of what happened?"

Mom sighs. "Well…"

"I'll take it, hun, why don't you, uh…"

"I'll clear the table," she says as she gives Dad a kiss on the cheek.

"Okay, son. Well, your Mom and I were just little kids at the time, but it's still a vivid memory for both of us, I'm sure. I was at school when it all happened. And it all happened very quickly."

"Didn't it take like almost two weeks, like, thirteen days or something?"

"No, no, this all happened in one day. I remember our teacher was getting updates on her radio and, then by noon, the administrators, they all hauled us into the auditorium. We didn't know what was going on. We were in grade school, just kids. Of course, I know what happened now. Everyone knows. I can still feel the tension in that room with the looks on all the teachers' faces. They kept us there 'till the bell rang. They didn't know what to do, whether we were in danger or not."

"So what happened, Dad?"

"Really, Jon, I'm sure your books can tell you more than I can."

"I know. I just want a quick rundown."

"Well, at first we thought it was minor. But as the day unfolded, when we got home that night, President Kennedy came on TV and told us what had happened. He announced that the Soviets had Intermediate Range Ballistic Missiles with nuclear warheads positioned in Cuba. As soon as he went on the air, as soon as he hit the airwaves, he was interrupted because six of the nukes were launched."

"At us?!?!" I ask in disbelief.

"Yeah, well, that's what we all thought. They were headed straight for Washington, Baltimore and New York. Two each. But at the last minute all six were diverted into the Atlantic Ocean, far enough away that they didn't affect anything, except the fish, of course."

"Well, that's good." I add.

"Yeah, that was good but, it made us focus on Cuba, when out of nowhere, and I mean nowhere, our entire West Coast was overrun by Soviet tanks, soldiers and ships; I mean you name it, they had it there. It was as if they were cloaked and just magically appeared all at once. I remember watching it on TV with your grandparents. The news reporters didn't know how to report it. We didn't know what we were watching. None of it showed up on radar. None at all. I know it sounds crazy, son, but it was as if they were just zapped or beamed there or

66

something."

"Beamed there instantaneously huh, Dad? That actually doesn't sound too crazy. It sounds ingenious."

So they got us all up in arms about nukes, focused on the East Coast and then attacked our West Coast with a ground invasion instead. That makes perfect sense, actually. Not only did it draw our attention, but it also drew our forces to Florida and the Southeast to be closer to Cuba. They didn't even have to do that since they had the time machine and all. We wouldn't have had a chance either way. The nukes just added some bark to their bite.

"Wow, Dad, that's crazy."

"Yeah. We didn't have a chance. Not at all. Every time we deployed new troops, the Soviets kept appearing one after another."

"So, why did they stop where they stopped? I mean, this may sound bad but, why not just take over the whole country? Why stop around the Mississippi?"

"Well, it was a natural place to stop I guess, easy to defend against. They destroyed the bridges and cut off all access to the West. I think it was more psychologically damaging to us this way, ya know, not taking over the entire thing. Letting us know that some of us are still free while a good majority of us are under their rule. Kinda just like East and West Berlin. I think the Soviets like to play cat and mouse with us, to see if we'll try to escape so they can

67

capture us again."

"Makes sense, I guess. So how did we respond?"

"Well, for one, Texas fought back. And I mean every Texan fought back. It's like the whole state mobilized and guarded their border. I guess they are used to protecting their borders, but this time it was more than just the South. And somehow, they were able to keep Texas intact."

"All of it?"

"Well, all but the panhandle, yeah. Texas became independent, just like they always wanted. Now it's the Republic of Texas. They have their own everything now, even president."

"Wow, so Kennedy was no longer their president?"

"Nope, he just ruled over the Eastern part of the nation, the remaining United States. He narrowly got reelected 'cuz some people thought he wasn't taking a hard enough stance against the Soviets. But he tried to make up for it during his second term. We made headway once. Kennedy's newly formed covert group, under the facade of the Peace Corps, infiltrated some Soviet bases from within. But, it didn't last. We have just kind of accepted it now, son."

"That's not the America I know! We don't back down at all, Dad! And…wait, did you say Kennedy's *second* term?"

"Yeah, two terms in office. Come on, son

you know all of this!"

Of course! If Texas was no longer part of the US, Kennedy would have had no reason to visit Dallas! He was never in Dealey Plaza and therefore was never assassinated. This is intense. Well at least one good thing came out of this.

"I know, Dad. It . . . it just makes more sense to me when I hear from others, ya know? It helps puts the pieces together a bit more."

"Yeah, Jon. I gotcha."

I finish a forkful of food, get up and tuck in my chair. Wiping my face with my napkin I say, "Thanks, Dad. Mom, I'm sorry about your family. I'm sorry that everything happened the way it did."

"Oh, Jon, you make it sound as if it were your fault. Come here." She extends her arms and pulls me in for a long and comforting embrace, a needed embrace, before our attempt to set things right.

"Okay, guys, big day of fishing tomorrow."

"Wow, Jonny, you sure have taken a liking to fishing recently," Mom says.

"Oh, yeah, ha-ha. Well, off to bed! Night!"

CHAPTER EIGHT

"What? What the . . . Feebz!"

Feeby's tongue licks my face for a seventh and eighth time before I realize what is happening.

"Hey, girl." I say as I sit up in bed and stretch my arms towards the ceiling. As I wipe the sleep from my eyes, I glance over at my DVD player to find out the time.

"Nine o'clock. Feebz, who needs an alarm clock with you around? You got me up right on time, once again, girl."

"Walllluuuu! Wallllluuuu!" Our bird call. It must be Pete.

I pull up the window shade to see Pete, sitting on his electric scooter and waving at me. I open the metal lock, lift the window and tell him I'll be down in one minute.

I quickly change, splash some water in my face and head downstairs.

"Morning, hun," says Mom as she carries up a load of laundry.

"I don't think I heard that shower running,

Jon."

"Uh, no ma'am. Not today. I took one last night before bed. Plus, I am just about to get all smelly from fishing again, ya know?"

"All right. Well, just this once. You have fun and tell your cousin I said hello."

"Will do, Mom," I say as I grab a handful of my favorite marshmallow cereal. Maybe I'll get some luck from the leprechaun on the front of the box. I head out the front door and meet Pete.

"Sup, Jonny boy!"

"Hey, Pete. Mom says, hey."

"Hi, Auntie Brewster!" he screams at the top of his lungs as I hop on the back of his scooter.

"Head to the bank." I say.

"I know. I know," he says as he accelerates to the scooter's maximum speed.

"I just texted Abby. She is finishing up at the thrift shop and will meet us at the plantation house."

"Sounds good." I say.

We make our way through the neighborhood, cut through the park and head to Main Street.

"You have the bank box key?"

"Yeah, sure do, Pete. You ready for this?"

"You know it, bro. At least this time I know what to expect!" he says.

"Very true my friend, very true!" I say, smiling back.

We continue our trek to town and pass Bobby Newton. He is carrying his favorite red fishing rod and tackle box, on his way to the lake.

"Bobby," I yell from the scooter as we continue to drive by, "Don't forget, we're with you all day, okay, man!"

"I got you covered, Jon! But hey, for real, come join me later!"

"Will do, bud! Thanks!" I yell.

We finally reach the bank. Pete keeps the scooter running as he and I both hope it will be a short stop.

I run inside, head to the enormous vault and find my box. It amazes me that the vault door is always left wide open like this. I mean, I know you need a key to get into the boxes, but still, I would feel a bit more assured if a one-of-a-kind time machine device were actually *locked up* behind that huge steel door. I wonder if it would be safer in the treehouse. Or, maybe I just watch too many movies about bank robberies.

I stick the key in the slot and retrieve the box. I set it on the counter and open it. Looking around, I make sure there are no Jackson or Klara-esque characters roaming around the bank. I reach inside the bag and pull out the primary device and the freeze ray. I shove them into the deepest pocket of my cargo shorts, put the bag back in the box and the box back in its slot. One turn of the key to lock it and I'm back out with Pete and his scooter. Pete starts the motor and accelerates us towards the plantation house where we're scheduled to meet up with Abby.

He cuts over a parking lot of an old, abandoned drive-in movie theatre. We bump across the gravel and pot holes and head for the other side. We take the dirt trail through the woods that backs up to the plantation house. In the distance I can see Abby standing on the back porch with Chuck. Her red hair shines in the sunlight. She waves with one hand and holds up a bag with the other.

Pete gives his engine an extra boost as we clear the tree line and bounce our way up to the back porch.

"Hey, guys, thought you weren't coming," Abby says as we pull up and dismount the scooter.

"I got some clothes." Abby opens the bag and lays everything on the two weathering rocking chairs with crackling white paint. Pete and I head up the rickety stairs and greet Chuck with a head nod and a wave.

"This is yours, Pete, and yours, Jon, and this is mine," she says pointing to three separate piles of clothes. "I just got here so I didn't have time to change yet."

"This one must be mine," Pete says as he picks up the pile Abby had called mine.

"No, Pete, those are Jon's. You have these, the green ones."

"What? But you know I dig blue. Why can't I have the blue shirt and blue jeans?"

"Cuz, that's for Jon. Now just take it!"

"Ah, it's okay, we're the same size, he can

73

have it," I say as I pick up the green pile of 1940's era clothes. We don't have any time to waste on the drama of what color clothes we're gonna wear. And here I thought they were getting to like each other.

"Whoa, whoa, whoa! What is this?" Pete says, shaking his head and holding up his pants.

"These are bellbottoms. Correct me if I'm wrong, but they didn't really have bellbottoms in the 40's!" he says.

"Sucks to be you, Pete! I told you the green pile was for you," says Abby as she looks over at me, smiles and shrugs her shoulders.

"Thanks, Abby," I say as she responds with a pair of duck lips.

"It'll have to do, Pete."

"Go ahead inside and change, guys." Chuck says. "Abby, you can use the bathroom to the left and Pete, the bedroom is to the right," Chuck says.

They go inside the plantation house. I stay outside with Chuck and start to change my shirt.

"Still got that scrawny bird chest, I see, ha-ha," says Chuck as I reach my arms over my head while taking off my shirt.

"Ha, shut up, Chuck. I would imagine so, it was only a few days ago."

"Yeah. That's true. So, are you ready for this, Jon?"

"Well, I mean, we have no choice really. We can at least try."

"I do apologize again, Jon," says Chuck

74

while shaking his head.

"No, no, if it's anyone's fault at all, it's Klara and Jackson's. Not ours," I say as I finish putting on the thrift store shirt.

"Well, I just wish I could do something more to help, is all. Wish I could go back with you, but who am I fooling... I can barely walk now-a-days, ha-ha."

"Yeah, I guess time travel would kinda be out of the question, huh?" We both laugh as Abby and Pete make their way back outside. Pete shoves Abby aside as he crams his way through the back door.

"Watch it, Pete!"

"Sorry, Abby. I had to get out of there." He turns to Chuck and says, "No offense, but this house creeps me out. I felt like someone was watching me the whole time I was in there."

"Well, it sure wasn't me," says Abby. "Probably nothing to see anyways!" she says as she winks and smiles at Pete.

"I'll be right back. Let me put these on," I say as I go inside. No time to go to another room, I simply stand behind the door and change, pulling my new vintage pants up over my shoes. Our shoes! We forget to get new shoes, too! Oh well, I guess we'll have to stick with our modern shoes. I finish changing, open the door and head back outside.

"Ready guys?" We all look at each other and

laugh.

"We look like we're actors in a low budget version of *West Side Story*," Abby says.

"It'll have to do. Come on, we gotta get going," I say, "Chuck, wish us luck!"

"Yeah, hope to see you soon, Chuck," says Pete

"Well, hope not to see you, that is," says Chuck.

"Whatcha mean?" asks Abby.

"If all goes right, everything will go back to normal, ya know? I won't live here anymore and well, everything will be back the way it was supposed to be before all of this happened."

"He's right," I say. "Well, Chuck, it was nice seeing you again. And, well, as bad as it sounds, I hope we never see you again, as well, ha-ha."

"Yeah, peace out, Chuck, ha-ha," Pete says as he slaps Chuck a high five.

"Well, maybe we can see you sometime, just visit us. Track us down again or something."

"Well, maybe I will, Abby. Maybe I will. Oh, almost forgot!" Chuck reaches in his right front pocket and pulls out a folded sheet of memo paper. "Here, this is the info you'll need once you make it to Chicago."

"Thanks, Chuck," I say as I shove the paper in my pocket.

Chuck takes a load off and retires in one of the rocking chairs. We finish with our goodbyes, double check that we have everything we need, step off the front porch and walk about ten yards away from the house.

"Okay, Jon, start'em up!" Pete says with an iffy smile on his face. I take the device out of the bag and prepare to pull the trigger.

"Jon, can I do it?" Abby says as she reaches for the device.

"Umm, I guess so, Abb. Go ahead, knock yourself out."

Abby takes the device with both hands and is careful not to drop it. She looks like she just discovered the golden ticket to the chocolate factory.

"Alright, guys! Here we go!" Abby says as she extends her pointer finger towards one of the square buttons on the front of the device.

"No, Abby! Not that! The trigger! The trigger!" I yell.

"Oh! Sorry! Here we go!" says Abby.

She flips the cover and pulls the trigger. Instantaneously we are blasted back to the past. The now familiar feeling of heat and cold rushes over us as the ground rumbles and shakes like Armageddon. The wind blows all around us as if a hurricane has just made landfall. My heart beats as fast as I feel it's possible and then slows down to almost a frozen state. Finally, my pulse and my other vitals reclaim their norm.

My blurry eyes start to clear up and things start to come into focus. As I begin to sit up, a huge explosion rocks the earth behind me and my ears begin to ring like after watching a rock concert from the pit. My eyes, once again blur up and sting with the brightness and heat of the explosion.

I lie on the pavement, covering my eyes and grasping my ringing ears as I begin to hear the faint sound of someone's voice. It sounds like they are calling my name. It must be Pete or Abby, but my ears, not to mention my head, are still ringing due to the explosion.

"Jon! Jon!" The voice clears up and comes to me. It almost sounds as if . . . no, no it can't be. It's not Abby or Pete calling for me. It's Chuck. Only, it's not 'old man Bailey' Chuck, it's *Chuck* Chuck!

CHAPTER NINE

"Jon! Take cover! Take cover!" I look around and find Abby to my left and Pete a few yards away stumbling around, dumbfounded, and rubbing his head. He must have gotten hit by something.

With my hearing fully recovered, I hear the unmistakable sound of a Japanese Zero roaring overhead and zipping by us. I push myself off the ground and reach out to Abby to help her up. Two more Zeros fly over and start to strafe the building adjacent to us.

"Jon! What happened? What happened?"

I grab Abby's hand and pull her away from the oncoming bullets of the Japanese pilot.

"I dunno, Abb! But we're obviously back at Pearl!"

Pete makes his way over towards us as we huddle together, keeping our heads down to avoid the debris being scattered throughout the air. We quickly, but cautiously, head over to Chuck.

"Holy . . . It's Chuck! Young Chuck!" Pete says as he realizes where we are. There's Chuck, standing in almost the exact same place as he was when we left. Only this time, Pete's not alone; we *all* have the same expression, one of confusion.

"Come on, guys! Take cover!" says Chuck as he waves us over. We press tightly along the side of what remains of the building. The windows that run along the top of the wall are all shattered. Pieces continue to fall to the ground along with chunks of cement and brick.

"I guess it didn't work?! You were only gone for a few seconds or so!" Chuck yells over the noise of war. "I'm sorry guys, I am . . ."

"No! No it *did* work Chuck, but, we just came back!" I say.

"What?" Chuck asks as two army jeeps come zipping around the corner of the building. The passenger of the first jeep fires his rifle at the planes above.

At the same time, Abby runs over to the burning wreckage of a Japanese Zero; it was the same Zero that almost crashed into us right before we left Pearl. I start running over to chase after her, but Chuck grabs my collar, preventing me from moving.

"What did you say?!" Chuck asks again.

I see Abby running back to cover with the temporal device in hand and feel a little more at ease.

"It worked!" I scream even louder. "But we came back, by accident!"

"What do you mean you came back?"

"Well, we had to come back. *You* actually

were the one who told us to come back."

"Yeah, man, it's all your fault, Chuck!" exclaims Pete as he casts a watchful eye to the sky.

"What, Pete? I can't hear you!"

" He means that . . ."

Once again, out of the blue we are no longer at Pearl. The sensation of time travel encompasses me, envelopes me. Abby must have hit the trigger again. I only pray to God that this time, it sends us to the right time and place.

The colors, the sounds, the heat and the cold remind me of an old 60's documentary on the effects of an acid trip. This time the temperature fluxuation is as intense as it ever has been. It feels like an eternity. I honestly don't know how much more I can take of this!

And just as soon as it started, it has completed its cycle. I am slammed onto the ground as if I were a kamikaze pilot. That was new.

Dazed and confused, I once again wipe the dizziness from my eyes.

For some reason these travels are getting more and more violent and unpredictably intense.

This time I spot Pete, but Abby is nowhere to be found. "Pete!" I yell out.

"Hey, man," he replies as he jogs over to me, rubbing his head. "Dude, that was rough! What just happened? I swear my head hurts more than any other time we used that thing," he says as he rubs his head. "Where are we, dude? And what was that all about? We were back in Hawaii!"

"No clue at all, man," I say as I push myself off the ground and look around. "I dunno. Could be a college campus I guess. I mean, I haven't been to many before and none in the 40's, but it could be."

We look around to find ourselves surrounded by old brick buildings in city-style street blocks. An occasional shrub of greenery, a well-placed water fountain and bus stop outline a strip of grassy area. I guess it could be a park in the middle of campus.

"Look at all the cars, Pete. I know you're the car guy, but these do look like 40's cars to me. Maybe we finally got here after that brief detour."

"Yeah, man, why did we go back to Hawaii? Did Abby push – Wait, where's Abby!?"

"I dunno, Pete. She's gotta be around here somewhere. Come on."

"Abby! Abbyyyyy!" Pete cries.

"Shut up, dude. We don't want to draw attention to ourselves! Come on, Pete! You'd think you'd know this by now."

"I know, I know, but where is she, man? I'm just, I mean, I just hope she's alright."

"Pete, why don't you just ask her out, already?" I ask while wiping some grass and leaves from my clothes.

"What?! You're . . . That's . . . You're crazy, man. I don't ... I mean . . ."

"Ha-ha, yeah, yeah. Well, if you don't ask her to homecoming this fall then I'll ask her for you!"

"She doesn't dig me, man. I mean . . . it's just . . . shoot, man. I dunno! It's so weird, ya know?"

"Ha, yeah, man. We can talk about that later. Here she comes." Abby casually walks down the sidewalk, comes to a corner, and waits for a taxi to drive by. She notices that we see her and waves as we start walking toward her. We meet up at the water fountain.

"Hello, boys! Anyone else feel like they were just shot across the globe with the catapult of death from *Mayhem Mountain,* Issue #17? What was that?"

I guess we all agree these time travel jaunts are inherently dangerous. But now they're getting more painful trip by trip.

"Where were you, Abby?" Pete asks as he taps her shoulder. She brushes her bright red hair out of her eyes and says, "Awww, did ya miss me, Petey?"

"Uh, . . .Nope! I just wanted to make sure we had the chance to blame you for sending us back to Pearl!" Pete says, blaming Abby.

"Hey, whatever! I did what you said. I pulled the trigger."

"No. No. You were messing around with one of those little square buttons on the front. Here," I say, "Let me see that thing."

I reach over as Abby hands me the device. I turn it around until I can get a clear look at the black square buttons. I don't see any labels, but as I rub my finger over one button that's still pushed in, I can feel some markings on it. The lettering has worn off, but as I bring it closer, I can see raised letters that say, "RECALL" and another button says "RANDOM."

That would be great. "Random." We could end up anytime, anywhere and any location at all. Just what we need. How did we not notice these before?

"Recall? Is that what it says?" asks Abby.

"Yeah," I say, handing it back to her. "I think we know what it does now."

"Jon, that's not right. As soon as you told me to pull the trigger and not to mess with those buttons, I let go of it. I wasn't pushing that button when we went back!"

"It doesn't matter, Abby. That's what happened, whether you wanted it to or not."

"Yeah, maybe it got stuck in that mode or something," Pete contributes.

Either way, this thing is acting up more now than ever. "Guys, I dunno how much longer we can trust this thing." I say.

"Who cares? We're here. Let's get the blueprints and leave." Pete says, while looking around at our new surroundings.

"No, I dunno guys. I think . . . I think we need to do something else before this thing totally destroys us, even before we try to save America."

"Yeah," Abby says as she reveals a burn on the palm of her hand.

"Ouch, Abby, what happened?" Pete says as

he looks intently at the wound.

"I'll be fine. It happened at Pearl when I found the device and picked it up. Funny thing is, it was as cold as ice. So, I guess it's like a really bad freezer burn or something."

"Yeah, that's fitting. 'Cuz you a cooooold bitch, Abby! Bahahaha!!" Pete says, trying to mask his concern over Abby's new wound.

"Whatever, jerk!" Abby slugs him in the belly. Pete folds over in a brief, but potent pain. "So what do you suggest, Jon?" she says as she consoles Pete and whispers, "Serves you right, jerk!"

"Well, you guys probably won't like it, but…I don't trust this thing. And every time we go somewhere new, something happens. We honestly know nothing about it, but we do know that ever since we found it, that thermal switch keeps messing up. I mean it shorts out all the time. It burned or froze Abby and it almost got us blown up by the Japanese again. It's basically holding us hostage!"

"Well, we have no other choice but to use it, Jon. We can't just go to the local electronics store and buy another one, now can we?" Pete says in a very dramatic and over the top robot voice.

"That's true, Mr. Roboto. But there is another one."

"Yeah, but the secondary is just a duplicate of the primary and it can only follow the first one," comments Pete. "Plus, we left it back at the bank."

"Wait . . . you don't mean the secondary one

85

do you, Jon?" Abby asks. "You mean the one that we are trying to prevent from being built!"

"Yup," I say shaking my head up and down and raising my eyebrows.

"But . . ."

"Wait, what?" asks Pete, dumfounded as always. "Sorry, guys. I'm not getting this."

"Pete, you need a time traveler's guide for the incompetent. I swear, man. Look at that thing," Abby says.

I hold the device up and reveal its wear and tear. It's singed and has a faint burning smell from within. I hold it up to my nose and sniff. "Look guys. Smell it!" Abby and Pete both take turns.

"Yeah," says Abby, "I guess it has seen better days."

"Well, I want to see better days too, back in our own time. This thing can die on us any minute now. We need something more reliable. I mean this thing is from the 40's and was never built properly to begin with. We can't risk not being able to get back."

"So, okay, you want us to go up in Chuck's dorm, steal the blueprints and then make the time device ourselves?"

"No, Pete, I don't think we could handle that at all."

"So what then?" Pete asks.

"We need to go back, or forward, to when the Russian made the time machine, tell him we know what he is planning, but tell him how much he will regret it and what actually happens. That way we stop him from messing up the Cuban Missile Crisis and get a brand new time machine to make sure we get back home."

"That's . . . that's intense man!"

"Jon," says Abby with her lips posed duck fashion, "Why don't we just find Chuck's dorm, get the blueprints and go back home like we planned?"

"Look at this thing! It's practically sizzling in my hand right now. Who knows how much longer it'll work! It could conk out it one minute and we would be stuck here forever!" I urge.

"Well, what if your plan doesn't work? We could be stuck somewhere *else* forever! I don't like it, Jon. Not at all!" admits Abby.

"Fine, let's vote on it." I say. "All in favor." Abby looks over at Pete as he reluctantly raises his hand. She gives him another hard punch, only this time, in the shoulder.

"Ouch! C'mon, Abby. Jon is a smart dude; I trust him."

"This is crazy! Ya know . . . Why not? Why not? Alright let's go then. What the hell?" Abby says, realizing she has lost the vote.

I pray that we have made the right decision. That *I* have made the right decision. I dunno, either way it's gonna be risky. "Alright guys."

"Next stop, Mother Russia!" says Pete in a thick Russian accent.

I look down at the device and slowly look

back up at Pete and Abby. "Well, I guess you can stop your worrying, Abby. It's out of juice."

"What? Well, we'll just have to recharge it somehow!" explains Pete.

"Sure, dumbass, we'll go to the nearest time travel store and buy a charger cable." Abby says, dismissing Pete's petty statement.

To which Pete responds, "Shut up, Abby! Nobody asked you! Besides, I already said we wouldn't be able to do something like that. Maybe if you would listen to me more often you would have heard me!"

"Okay, okay, guys." I say trying to bring a sense of calm back to the group. "There goes my plan. Well, at least part of it. I guess we'll have to do what we were gonna do in the first place."

"What do you mean, Jon?"

"Well, Pete, we still need to get the Russian, um, Vasily, to build us a new time machine. He will just have to build it a little bit earlier than expected."

CHAPTER TEN

We decide to make our way over to Chuck and Vasilys' dormitory. I notice that Pete is hunched over and looking all around as if he was an old-school robber on the lookout for keystone cops. I tell him to act inconspicuous and then remember who I am talking to and change my request by telling him to simply, "act normal."

I don't know why he is acting like this; I think we are blending in fine, considering these outfits we have on.

We walk along a campus path adjacent to South Ellis Avenue and pass by the *C bench*, a popular hangout for students, which is positioned right outside *Cobb Lecture Hall*. I explain that the bench has been there for over a hundred years, and was a gift to the University from the graduating class of 1903.

It's nothing special when you look at it. It's basically a big cement block in the shape of the letter *C*, hence the name, *C bench*. But once you enter *C bench*, it comes to life. Every word you say, no matter how soft, no matter how gentle, is amplified

89

tenfold. They really should have called it "*C echo bench*."

After explaining it to Pete, he, of course, has to try it out. I am hesitant and would prefer to get on with things sooner rather than later, but I know Pete needs his distractions in our time travel excursions. They help him sort things out a bit in his head.

The three of us decide to enter the partial cement circle. We scare away a kissing couple on one end, but a very studious collegiate sitting on the top of *C bench* stares intently at his textbook. I don't think he's going anywhere anytime soon. Abby and I take a seat while Pete stands in the center.

"Okay, so say something, Pete," declares Abby.

"Ummm, like, what should I say? Ha-ha!"

"I dunno just say something!"

"Okay," Pete says as he readies himself. He clears his throat and says, "My hoagie lives on Liberty Laaaaaaane!!!"

"What . . . was . . . that?" I ask as Pete's saying reverberates throughout *C bench*.

"First thing that came to my mind. I'm hungry, I guess."

"Yeah," Abby says, "But hoagies don't technically *live* anywhere. And if they did, I am sure they would not live on any *Liberty Lane*. Maybe *Hoagie Lane* or something? I –"

"Ha, come on you guys," I say as I take out the instructions Chuck gave me. "Ok, Chuck said we

90

need to head this way towards the main quadrangles. That's where we'll find his dorm, *Snell-Hitchcock Hall.* Hopefully, we'll find the Russian as well."

We continue towards the quadrangles and the center of campus. On our way there, as we do our best to blend in, we come across many students, hustling and bustling around campus. Surprisingly it's the middle of summer.

Now that I think about it, I guess more of them are enjoying recreational activities over studying. There are about ten guys in an open area throwing a football around, a guy and his girlfriend hold hands while hailing a taxi and a younger student shows his mom, dad and little sister around campus by identifying the various sights and points of interest.

And to think, all of this is happening while the world's first nuclear reactor, *Chicago Pile-1,* is being constructed underneath the grandstand of *Stagg field.* These students have no idea of the future historical importance of their college campus.

"Wow, guys! Can you believe the significance of this place? I mean, some of the world's top scientists, the start of the Manhattan Project . . . it just amazes me!" I say as we cross the street.

"Yeah, and, what if the first controlled nuclear reaction became *uncontrolled*; what then?" says Abby, giving Pete and me a wide grin.

"I know right! What if it explodes and the

whole campus goes up, or, or what if, what if the radiation leaks and, and like, all the students become zombies. They would have to rename it the *University of Zombies at Chicago*! Ha-ha! Aw, man, wait. That actually could happen!"

"But it didn't happen, Pete." says Abby with a hand on her hip, one of her most feminine, yet immature poses.

"Ahhh, Abby, but it could! Muhahahahha!" Pete says in his best Bela Lugosi, Dracula-styled voice.

"Look, there it is." I say as we finally reach the dormitory. We do our best to blend in and casually walk up the steps and enter the dorm. Good thing this is the past and not the future. Now-a-days, students need security cards to enter most dorms. They swipe them in a slot like a hotel room lock.

After taking another glimpse of the note Chuck gave us, we find the stairwell and head up to the third floor. Pete takes the lead, double-timing every other step, almost running over a coed on her way down the stairs. "Oh, my bad!" he says as he nods to her.

"My bad?" Abby says, once again shaking her head.

"Well, what did you want me to say . . . 'Many apologies my lady?'"

"How about a simple, I'm sorry!" Abby says as she shoves Pete through the third floor door. Pete looks back at Abby and hisses at her while clawing the air like a cat.

We enter the third floor corridor and cautiously walk towards Chuck's dorm room.

"Hey, guys, what if we get chased by one of those zombie students and we have to run back and forth all over the hallway from room to room? It would totally be like one of those funny old episodes of *Scooby Doo*! Ha-ha! Right? Right, you guys?" Pete says.

"Yes, yes, you're, right Pete. Geez and I'm the youngest of all of us." Abby says, shaking her head.

"Shut up, Abby!" says Pete, as he pushes her aside.

"Guys, here's the dorm," I say as we round the corner to the next hall. I put my hand on the knob and take a final look left and right down each side of the hallway. I slowly turn the knob only to find out the door is locked.

"Any ideas, guys?"

"Just break it down, Pete!" says Abby.

"No, man, someone might be in there. I'll . . . I'll just knock, okay? And if someone answers, we were mistakenly knocking on the wrong door."

"Well, what if Chuck answers?"

"Then we don't have anything to worry about now do we, Abby?" I say.

"Alright, let's do it!" Pete says, with his eyes wild and wide opened as if he really thinks a zombie is on the other side of the door.

I raise my arm, pull my fist back and knock three times. I wait five seconds then knock again. Still nothing.

"So, now what?" asks Abby.

"I zink you know vat vee have to do!" Pete says in a German accent. Or was it a *Dracula* accent? I'm really not sure this time.

"Yeah," I say, "We have to break in."

"Shouldn't be that hard, Jon," says Pete as he pulls out his gym card from his wallet. "Here, scoot over."

"Do you know what you're doing, Pete?" I ask

"Well, I have never done it before, but, I mean, how hard can it be?"

Pete approaches the door and gently slides his card in between the door and door jam in the area right next to the handle. With a couple of swipes up and down and a jiggle of the doorknob, the door opens.

"Open Sesame!" he says, as we quickly but quietly sneak inside.

The dorm room is your average dorm room, small, with standard furnishings and needless to say, average smell. No posters or crazy lighting. No computers or TVs or mini fridges like today's typical dorm. But, nevertheless, it's easy to tell it's a dorm: two beds, two dresser drawers and two desks.

"Alright, guys, start looking," I say as I head over to the window and draw the curtains shut.

"Jon, we kinda need that light." Abby says.

"Yeah, just hit the switch."

"Got it," says Pete as he turns on the lights and surveys the room for a place to start. I begin to look around in what I presume to be Chuck's side of the room. I can identify it as such because of three photos taped on the wall above his bed: one of his father and mother, one of his high school graduation and one of a giant palm tree with the sun setting in the background.

I start off by lifting up the mattress. Why not, right? It's been a great hiding place for years. Since it's only the 40's, I'm pretty sure I won't find any dirty magazines under here.

My search is interrupted by some commotion from Pete.

"Oh . . . my . . ."

"What is it, Pete? I ask.

"Did you find the blueprints?" asks Abby, as I drop the mattress and head over towards the other desk.

"You guys, . . ." Pete continues, "Holy-. . . are you serious?"

95

CHAPTER ELEVEN

And there, casually laid out on the Russian's desk next to a stack of Physics books, an apple core and a bag of licorice, rests the dream of every comic collector: *Action Comics #1*. Dated 1938, the cover displays Superman lifting an old green sedan, and saving the day.

"First appearance of Superman! First appearance of Superman!" Pete says as we stand there salivating. We are in comic geek heaven.

"Jon! Abby! This thing just sold at auction for almost two-million dollars! And here it is, right before us, in mint condition! I don't know about you guys, but I'm starting to like this Soviet agent!"

"Now, you're talking, Pete!" Abby says as she slowly and tactfully picks up the comic book.

"Let's take it! Come on, please, Jon! Let's take it! We could be rich! He would never miss it! Look!" Pete says as he points to a pile of other comics in a box underneath the desk. "Please, please, please!"

For a second I think to myself, yes, we have to! But alas, we can't.

Pete whispers to himself, "Don't say no! Don't say no! Don't say no!"

"Sorry, Pete," I pause and sigh, "But we just can't do it, man. Believe me I would love to. It would just change too much."

"Aw, man! I am so sick of these stupid time traveling rules and morals and crap. Here we are saving the world, AGAIN and we can't even get rewarded for it!" Pete says as he watches Abby put the comic book back on the desk.

"I know, dude, but we just can't. Now come on! Find the blueprints! Staaaaaaay focused!" I say as lose my own focus and stare at the comic book.

We spread out again, as much as we can in the tiny quarters, and continue our search, much to the chagrin of Pete and his millionaire comic book fantasy.

"Oww! Darn it!" Abby cries from the front of the room.

"What's up, Abby?" I ask.

"Ahh, I hit my foot on something under the bed, something really hard."

"You know what's hard for me to grasp? Knowing that we could be millionaires with one simple comic book and not doing anything about it!"

"Peter!"

"Alright, alright," Pete says as he glances back at the comic.

"What was it Abby?" I ask.

"You guys!" she says as she rubs her toes

through her shoe, "Check this out!"

Pete and I walk towards Abby as she peers under the bed. To our surprise the culprit was a small, cast-iron lock box. It's like a safe but a little more portable. Well, not that portable; it's still pretty heavy.

"Dude, a lock box? Like Al Gore, 'I'm gonna put it in a lock box,'" Pete says in a very lame attempt at a Gore impression. I am honestly surprised Pete knows anything about Al Gore at all.

"You guys thinking what I'm thinking?"

"It has to be, Abby. We searched everywhere else already. And what better place to hide it, ya know?"

"Yeah, Jon, but only one problem: It's a lock box, so, it's, ya know, kinda locked."

"True that." I reply.

"Let's smash it! Find a hammer or something or a drill!" Pete says as he flexes some muscle and picks up the box.

"Sure Pete, 'cuz every dorm has one of those."

"Well, at least I'm trying! You got any brighter ideas, Abby?"

"Shoot, I dunno . . . Jon?"

"Actually, I do. I brought the freeze ray remember?" I remind them both.

"That's right! Good idea, man. Just be careful 'cuz you know what happened last time, ha-ha."

"Yeah!" I agree.

I reach in my pocket and pull out the freeze ray. We pause and stare at it while being mesmerized by its majestic cobalt frame. Snapping out of it, I turn the dial on the handle. Doing so illuminates the trigger with a pulsing blue glow. Von Wexler sure did have a thing for internally illuminating his inventions.

"Okay, guys! Stand back!" For our own safety, I turn the dial to its lowest setting. Pete places the lock box on the floor in front of us while I take aim.

"I hope this works! I'm only gonna give it a quick shot. We don't want to damage the blueprints if they are actually in there," I say as I squeeze my eyes and pull the trigger.

A blast of freezing cold surrounds us as the beam of ice wrecks through the lock box, shattering it to pieces. But unlike the first time when Pete and I demolished our cherished SR-71 Blackbird model, the ray only blew the box into a few big chunks instead of hundreds of little pieces. I guess it was good that I put it on its lowest setting. Plus, the box was made of a more durable material then our cheap plastic model. Good thing, too. We need those blueprints or we're out of luck.

"Look! I knew it!" screams Pete.

"Shhhh, quiet, man!"

"Oh. Sorry. But look! The blueprints!"

"Yeah, good job stubbing your toe, Abby!" I

jest with an added smirk.

I pick up the blueprint pages, the very same pages that will complete Deitrick Von Wexler's blueprint book, the very same pages that Chuck snatched from us back in Oahu and the very same pages that will bring us home!

"We got 'em!" I say.

"Great! Now we just gotta find Russian boy and get him to build us a new one and go back home!" Pete says, with a grimace.

"Russian boy? You've found him" says a tall, dark-haired twenty something standing in the doorway. We didn't hear him open the door with all the excitement and focus on finding the blueprints.

"Vasily!" Abby says as the Russian turns around peeks out into the hallway, looks left and right and quietly shuts the door.

"Now. Who are you and how do you know who I am? Nobody here knows the name Vasily, not even my roommate!"

"Chuck! Yeah, where is Chuck anyways?"

"Quiet, Pete," says Abby.

"You know of Charles, as well? Who are you guys? Well, I guess I no longer have to fake this American accent around you." He quickly seems more comfortable and less quirky as he assumes his own vernacular.

"The blueprints! Hand those over!"

"No way, dude! They're not yours!" Pete says as he prepares to throw fists to save the schematics.

"That may be true, but they are not yours either!"

"So why did you take them from Chuck then?"

"So you know they are Charles'? Did he send you here to retrieve them? I had no idea he even knew they were missing. I just took them the other day!"

"He doesn't. I mean, he does. Chuck does, that is to say, but . . . not this Chuck. I mean . . ." Pete says, confusing himself.

"You make no sense at all! I want answers and I want them now! How do you know who I am?" Vasily says, infuriated.

"Knock, knock," says a familiar voice on the other side of the door, while actually knocking.

"Chuck!" Abby cries.

"Good! Now we can get this whole story out once and for all," says Vasily as he unlocks the door and refrains from blocking it.

"Hey, sorry, Oliver. I heard voices and didn't want to interrupt, but I just forgot my . . . Jon! Pete! Abby!!!??? You guys!! What are you doing here?!!"

"No more secrets, Charles, I know you know why they're here, and don't bother calling me Oliver anymore."

"Huh? Guys, what are you doing here? And what is he talking about? How do you guys know Oliver?"

"Enough with the charades, man. You know my name is Vasily."

"Vasily? Ha-ha, yeah right. Sounds like a Commi name to me, man. Ha-ha. Vasily. Next thing you're gonna say is that you were sent here by the Kremlin to steal our nuclear program. Ha-ha!" Chuck says while slapping his leg.

"Not to steal it, to help you build it, you idiot!" says Vasily.

"Yeah, well you *did* steal the blueprints!" Abby says.

"Blueprints?!" Chuck hurriedly goes over to his desk and opens the bottom right drawer. He removes a huge stack of papers and folders and then lifts up a false bottom, obviously where he had hidden the blueprints.

"You dirty little . . . You're a thief!" Chuck cries, his face getting redder by the second.

"Takes one to know one, Chuck!" says Abby, giving him the good old duck lips.

Chuck regains his cool at the realization that his original theft of the blueprints has been discovered. "Oh. Oh, yeah. Guys, I'm sorry. I really am!"

"No need, Chuck, no need." I console.

"Yeah. Besides you already apologized up and down for taking them, and it was quite a spectacle, man. We don't wanna see you getting all emotional again," Pete says as he mocks Chuck bringing his hands to his eyes as if wiping back tears.

102

"Dude, he was like 100 when he apologized. How can you make fun of him like that?" I say.

"Yeah. True. Sorry, Jon," says Pete.

"Whoa, guys, I never apologized, what are you talking about?" asks Chuck.

"Yes!" says Vasily, "Start explaining yourselves now!"

"Slow your role, Boris! Take a sssssswig of vodka why don't ya. I know you have sssssome around here somewhere." Pete says in a slurring, drunkard, voice.

"Ha-ha! Same old, witty Pete!" Chuck says with a smile, forgetting that he was just found with his proverbial hand in the cookie jar, not to mention that his roommate is a Soviet spy.

"Okay, everyone take a seat." I order.

"Yeah, man, my back is still killing me from that last travel." Pete says.

"Well, now is a good time for us to rest. It's gonna take a long time to explain all of this."

"Wait," Vasily interjects. "When you say, travel . . . you don't mean . . .?"

Pete replies in his old gold prospector voice, "Hold onto your hat, comrade. We're talkin' bout tiiiiiiiiiiiiime traaaaaaaaaaaavel!!"

CHAPTER TWELVE

"Time travel? Are you serious? I mean, I know I took the blueprints and all, but deep down, I didn't think it was possible and, honestly, I just took them as a joke, but . . . you're telling me-"

"Oh, it's possible," Abby tells Vasily.

"Yeah, and we're here to prove it, too!" says Pete, licking the tip of his right index finger and pressing it against his skin, making a sizzling sound. I guess he means we are hot out of the space-time continuum? But knowing, Pete, he probably doesn't even know what he means by that.

Chuck is still in utter amazement. "You guys, I still can't believe it's you! I thought I would never see you guys again, and here you are, just a few years later, but you look the same. When you guys came back only a few seconds after you had left at the bombing of Pearl, I thought something happened. I thought that busted old device didn't work at all. But then you vanished again. And now . . . now you're back again!"

"Oh, when we came back a few seconds after we left Pearl. Yeah, that just happened!" I explain.

"Just happened?"

"Yeah, like, thirty minutes ago."

"No, no, that was over a year ago, almost two years, even."

"Well, it was for *you*, but it was just a half hour ago for us, Chuck. You know, time travel and all," says Abby.

"We had some malfunctions with the device. That damned thermal switch again," I add.

"Well, leave it up to us to rely on a Nazi invention," says Pete.

"Ha-ha, yeah. So, why did you come back? Why are you back here now? I'm guessing something happened with the blueprints, right? And how does my roommate play a part in all of this?"

"You mean, you really don't know about me, Chuck?" asks Vasily.

"Well, I'm starting to put it all together now, I think. Are you some kind of Commi spy or something!?" Chuck says with fist raised.

"Calm down, Chuck," says Abby. "Geez, I think I like the 'old man Chuck' better!" she says.

"Old man Chuck? Okay, guys, please start from the beginning."

"Yes, please do. I insist," says Vasily.

"Well, as I said, it's gonna take a long time. So sit back and relax."

Just then comes a knock on the door, that's already slightly ajar.

"Hello, boys? I heard some commotion. Everything okay?"

105

"Oh hey, Trish. Yeah we were just carrying on with some friends. Sorry about that," says Chuck.

"No problem, boys. You know it's summertime. No need to stress! Finals are months away!"

"Guys, this is Trish, our resident advisor for our hall. Trish, this is Abby, Jon and Pete, my friends from . . . umm, Hawaii."

"I was gonna guess Hawaii. You all have some weird fashion styles out there, huh?" Trish comments.

Pete gently steps on Abby's foot to remind her that she was the one who picked out the clothes.

"Shut up, Pete! I did the best I could with the time we had." Abby says.

"Okay. Well, enjoy the windy city. I'll see ya around," Trish says as she closes the door and walks away.

"Who was that again? She was kinda hot!" Pete says while nodding to Chuck.

"Yeah, she just kinda organizes events in the hall and makes sure everything is going okay. Ya know, to keep kids outta trouble."

"Ha, I'm sure she could help me get into some trouble, ha-ha. Naw' mean!"

"Shut up, Pete!" says Abby, shaking her head.

As they calm down, everyone sits and listens as I explain everything and I mean *everything* from the beginning. I explain how the device was found, how we went back to the eve of that infamous attack on Pearl Harbor, how we met Chuck and eventually how we returned.

I explained how 'old man' Chuck contacted us just a week after our return to tell us how things went wrong. And that his college roommate took vengeance on the US by using the Cuban Missile Crisis, back in '62, as a decoy, and using the time machine to attack the West Coast of the United States.

I also told them how we came back to retrieve the blueprints to make sure another one was never built.

Chuck sprawls out on his bed and takes a dazed look outside his window. A bluebird flies onto the windowsill and chirps. It's a very serene view after a not so serene explanation. But it doesn't last long as Vasily lets out a huge cry while banging both fists on his desk. The bluebird flies away as quickly as it got here.

"I can't believe they are not going to give me asylum! I can't believe it! I love America. I DON'T want to go back to Russia. Not Now! Not Ever!" Vasily shakes his head, gets up and begins to pace the small dorm room. "But still, I don't believe I could do such a thing. Use the time machine to help attack America? That's crazy!"

"Remember, man, it wasn't your intention. Khrushchev and the Politburo just took it too far. They took full advantage of having such a powerful device," I console. "And also, the future is not written yet! We can change things, ya know?"

Vasily sits down at his desk, wipes the tears of anger and disappointment from his eyes and looks directly at me.

"Jon, as sad as it makes me know that I will not be able to remain in the states, I promise you, all of you, I will not make another time machine."

"Oh, well, actually, I guess I left that little part out. Uh, we kinda, I mean, we would really appreciate it if . . ."

Abby grabs the temporal device from my pocket, raises it in the air and says, "Ours is broke! So, you need to build a new one so we can get home. Got it? Got it?"

"Thanks, Abby," I say while reaching out my hand and retrieving the device.

"So, yeah, we kinda need your help. You need to make it." I say.

"And we need to take it! Ha-ha!"adds Pete.

"Of course I don't want you to be stuck here away from your family and friends and your own life and time. But, I am not sure I can do it. I mean, you said I built one after the event called the Cuban Missile Crisis in 1962. That's twenty years from now. I *just* took the blueprints. I thought it was a joke. And now, you're not only telling me it really works, that time travel is possible, but that I need to build this for you, some twenty years ahead of when I actually build it?"

"Come on," says Chuck, "you've gotta have some kind of smarts already if you're a Soviet over here in the states, working for the US government on loan from Moscow."

"I didn't say I couldn't do it. It's just . . . it will just take some time is all.

"Ha-ha, time! Get it guys, time? 'Cuz we're talking about time travel and he said he needs some time! Well, . . . get it?"

"Yes! Yes we get it, Pete," says Abby, shaking her head.

"Shut up, Abby!"

"Look, guys," says Chuck. "I have studied those blueprints time and time again and with what I know, what he knows and the flaws that you three have experienced, I think we can do it." Chuck stands up and heads towards the door. "We just need to get some of my notes over at the research facility. I think we can do it guys. Once again, sorry I got you guys into this mess."

"Yeah, no worries, man," I say as Chuck opens the door.

We start to head out. I turn back and catch a glimpse of Pete.

"Peter!" I scold.

"Damn it!" Pete says as he removes the Superman comic from underneath his shirt and puts it back on the desk.

"Sorry, Jon."

We head out into the poorly lit hallway,

where we once again find Trish, right outside our door.

CHAPTER THIRTEEN

"Hello again. Taking them out for a little tour I see?"

"Yeah," says Chuck, "Um, we may go downtown, grab a hot dog or two from a vendor, show them around, ya know?"

"Okay. Well, have fun!" Trish says.

We continue to walk down the hall and make our way to the stairwell.

"You know, as long as I've been here, I still have not tried one of these hot dogs." says Vasily. "Pizza, yes. Hot dog, no."

"You've never had a hot dog!" Pete exclaims. "What are you, some kinda Commi!" Then realizing what he said, says, "Oh. Oh, yeah. You are. Ha-ha! Sorry!"

Vasily looks at Abby and me for an explanation. Abby just shakes her head while I shrug my shoulders.

"So what is it like in Russia, anyways?" asks Pete.

"Oh you know, the usual: stale bread and potato and an occasional, daily military parade."

111

"Ha-ha, quit playing . . . oh, for real?"

Vasily and Chuck continue to lead the way. We exit the dorm building and head towards the research facility. During the entire trip, Pete constantly bugs Vasily about topics including Russia, Communism, Russian women and what it's like being a spy. To which Vasily quickly replies, "I'm no spy. I am just here undercover to help you guys build the bomb before the Nazis do! Okay?"

"You know what the funny thing about that is?" I ask. "We don't even end up using the atomic bomb on Germany."

"What?!" screams Vasily, "That is impossible! Then why am I wasting my time here?"

"Just wait for it, Oliver. I mean, Vasily." says Chuck, still adjusting to his roommates 'new' name.

"Yeah, let him finish," adds Pete.

"We drop it on Japan, two times over." I say.

"The Japanese? Wow! I am sure Stalin will like that. We have had hard feelings towards Japan since the loss of the Russo-Japanese War in 1905."

Vasily slows his pace and looks towards the sidewalk. "Damn," he says, "I guess I have to be prepared for life under Stalin once more. I still can't believe the Americans don't end up giving me asylum."

"Well, was life really that bad under . . ."

"Pete! Think before you speak!" says Abby.

"Oh, yeah. Stalin. Right." Pete acknowledges.

112

"Yes, well, most of my family on my mother's side, or at least a good portion of them, were decimated during the great purge of 1937. Needless to say, my opinion of 'Mother Russia' has changed a lot since then."

We shake our heads in agreement while crossing over two side streets and taking a short cut through an alley.

We finally arrive at the facility. Chuck opens the door and leads us down a narrow hallway, just to the left of the main entrance.

The walls are covered with bulletin boards, posts of all sorts of campus information, especially pertaining to the subjects of physics, chemistry and engineering. We follow Chuck to the end of another long corridor where a security guard is seated. Chuck and Vasily sign in and present their ID cards.

"We'd like to show my guests around for a little bit, if that's alright, Henry."

"Well, I'm not really supposed to, but since it is summertime and you boys are stuck here studying hard, I guess it'll be okay for a little bit. But just enough time to show them around, okay? Don't go trying to invent some new-fangled, space-aged surfboard wax or something!" Henry chuckles a hearty chuckle.

"Ha, you know me too well, Henry!" Chuck says as he signs us into the log.

"Alright boys, there ya go," says Henry as he unlocks the set of blue steel double doors that lead to

113

the next hallway.

"I'll be here waiting for ya."

"Thanks, Henry," says Vasily.

"He's a really nice guy," Chuck says as we continue to follow his lead down the hall.

"Okay, this is it," Chuck says as he pulls a crowded key ring from his pocket, finds the correct key and sticks it in the door.

The door opens and reveals a very large workroom with an adjoining laboratory. Vasily hits the switch and the entire area is illuminated with the familiar buzzing hum of incandescent bulbs.

It's an enormous room, about half the size of a football field. Each section has its own desk, chair, basic tools, as well as other unidentifiable scientific instruments. There are hanging power cords and cables running all along the wall. A very primitive looking computer, reminiscent of the ENIAC, lines the entire back wall.

"Here. My space is over here," Chuck says, leading us to the middle of the room.

At his desk, he unlocks his top right drawer and retrieves a blue notebook. "Here it is," he says. He thumbs through the pages of notebook paper, tears out one page and hands it to Vasily.

"Oliver, uh, Vasily, get these for me. We're gonna need them."

"Why can't we just make it here?"

"No, you heard what Henry said. In and out. Come on! Get going." Chuck insists.

Vasily heads to the back of the immense room towards another set of doors, presumably a stock closet.

Chuck continues to thumb through his notepad. He spots another page of information that he needs, and using it as a reference, grabs some tools from a nearby desk. He also grabs a bag from his bottom right drawer and begins to shove the items inside.

"Chuck, I feel like we're stealing all of this stuff. Won't somebody suspect us, walking out of here with all this?" Abby asks, pensively.

"We'll leave through another exit." Chuck explains.

"But, Henry will know we didn't sign out."

"Ah, he could care less. He's probably out there dozing off already. And I would, too. What a boring job."

"Here comes Vasily!" Abby says as we turn and see him with a box full of items, including a primitive welding gun that is precariously placed on top.

"Good," says Chuck.

"I got it all, Chuck. Good thing we needed it during summer and not during the fall semester. They must have just stocked up."

"That's great! Here, Pete." Chuck transfers some items from Vasily's box into Pete's arms.

"That it? That everything?" I ask. Chuck reviews all the items on his checklist and says,

"Yup." He throws the blue notebook into the box, and we head towards a side door exit. Chuck looks around the corner to make sure the coast is clear.

"Hey, where's Henry?" asks Chuck as he does a double-take and peers around the corner.

"Who cares? We're going this way, right?" asks Pete.

"Yeah but he may sneak up on us or something." corrects Abby.

"Yeah, something is up. He never leaves that . . . Oh, no! Oh, my . . ."

"What is it, Chuck?"

"He's on the ground under the desk. Let's go!"

Chuck hands me his supplies and likewise Vasily hands his to Peter. They both take off ahead of us and run down the hall. We quickly file around the corner one by one, supplies in hand, following their lead.

Chuck bends over behind the desk and calls out Henry's name, while gently shaking him.

"Is he? Is he . . .?"

"No, Abby. He's still breathing and still has a pulse, thank God," Chuck reassures.

"So what happened to him, then?" asks Pete. "Is he just sleeping?"

"Yes, you could say that."

"Trish! What are you doing here? What have you done to Henry?!" exclaims Chuck.

Trish stands there, hands on her hips. This

doesn't look good.

"He'll be okay; it was a mild sedative, that's all."

"Mild sedative!" Abby says while kneeling down over Henry, observing a heavy black and blue bruise. "More like a wop on his head, you twisted witch!"

"Who are you and what do you want?!" demands Chuck.

"Yeah, and why do you sound different now? *Now* you have an accent!" I add.

"Well, you know what that means, guys. When someone starts using a different voice, it usually means we're out of luck!" Pete adds.

"Yes, I am Russian, just like Vasily," says Trish, "But I see you already know that. I was sent here to watch over Vasily, to make sure he didn't get any crazy ideas, kind of like what you are up to right now."

"I thought I saw a bottle of Vodka in your trashcan the other night! Vodka that is a little hard to get here in the states." Vasily says.

"Yes, well, I am your keeper, so to speak and sometimes this job drives me crazy you know!"

"What a perfect cover, being a resident advisor and being able to look over me all the time. I should have known they would not have trusted me to do things on my own. Thanks again, Mother Russia."

"Yes, and we will thank Mother Russia by

building that device and doing what you did in the first place!"

"What, uh . . . , what are you talking about?"

"I overhead everything back in the dorm. I like that story about how the Soviet Union takes over half of the United States. And I intend on keeping it that way!" Trish declares.

"No, way! We came back here to prevent that from happening, to set things right, how they were supposed to be in the first place! What makes you think we'll do it for you?" I question.

"Boys," she says while looking behind her. Two giants of men, wearing grey flannel business suits appear out of nowhere and cast an even darker shadow of despair in the hall. They look like they could have just signed a contract with the local big and tall shop. These guys are huge.

"And if *their* guns don't impress you, I have a set of my own." She pulls up her shirt to reveal a revolver. She then lifts the bottom of her pants to reveal another firearm strapped to her ankle.

"Of course, bad guys always have guns! We couldn't have just the two huge Russian men of steel, she had to have guns too. I'm sure they are strapped as well. Nice." Pete says.

"Just think, my name, Valentina Orlov, will be right there with Marx, Engles, Lenin and Stalin! I will be first famous female Soviet. I will not have to work my way up the ranks. This will guarantee me position in Politburo immediately!"

"No! Never!" screams Vasily.

"Come on, you heard your future friends here. You are not going to be granted political asylum! This country hates you after all your help in building secret bomb! Come back to Russia and we will make glorious future together!"

"Yeah, the *great* Russia that purged my family!?"

"Vasily, you know every cake takes a few broken eggs. Collateral damage is all. Your family will go down in history!"

Now I thought *Klara* was crazy. But this chick . . . go down in history? The millions of Russians that were ruthlessly murdered and she calls them collateral damage! Vasily is right at being infuriated by these demeaning remarks.

"Collateral damage! You're heartless!" cries Abby.

"Yeah, even I know that millions of defenseless people were killed just because your precious Stalin had a few screws loose!" says Pete.

At this statement one of her two henchmen gets heated and pushes towards Pete.

"No, it's okay, it's okay, Yuri."

"Yea, Yuri, it's okay! Did I hurt your feelings? Have a special place in your heart for Stalin, huh? Baby gonna cry? At least you don't have a dumb mustache like he does!"

"Cool it, Peter!" I say, putting my hand on his shoulder.

"Yes, cool it before I knock your block off, my little friend," says Yuri.

"Ha-ha! Ya sure his name isn't Igor, instead!" Pete jests. "I will knock block off!" he says with an exaggerated and slow Russian accent.

"Get in there and build that damned thing!" Trish, or should I say, Valentina, says as she motions to the entrance of the facility.

We all begrudgingly enter the laboratory, with supply in hand. I guess it will be easier to build it in here, after all. Although, I would prefer to build it under less strenuous conditions. The only thing I can hope for now is that we build it, and then somehow get rid of the three evil Russkies.

She motions us to go over to Chuck's desk and says, "Okay, you have what you need. Get to work. We will be keeping close eye on you and your friends so don't try anything funny, alright?"

Chuck and Vasily begin to empty the contents of the boxes around his workspace, as I help. Pete and Abby remain about ten yards away under close supervision of the two Ivan Drago look-a-likes. All I can picture them saying is the famous quote from *Rocky IV*, "If he dies, he dies." I am sure that is their sentiment exactly regarding my two best friends.

CHAPTER FOURTEEN

We continue to work on a new temporal device and are about halfway done. It's our third hour but feels like we've been working all day. I guess time slows down when a gun is aimed at you and your friends. Oh, wouldn't Klara and Jackson be proud of us now?

I tell Chuck and Vasily anything they need to know and act as an advisor, filling in the blanks to their questions about the time device and of its flaws, namely the thermal switch. I also tell them about its constant power fluctuation and the recent physical pain it has put us threw on our last couple of trips.

Pete and Abby are still under the eagle-eye supervision of the trio of Russians and needless to say, Pete doesn't look too happy. I just hope he doesn't try anything stupid.

"Yo, you guys almost done? We got Paul Bunyan and Goliath creepin us out over here!" he says.

"Just cool it, Pete. Cool it," says Chuck. "We're going as fast as we can, buddy!"

121

"Shut up and keep working. I am sick and tired of waiting," Valentina says as she pulls a cigarette from her pocket and snaps at Yuri for a light. He quickly responds and flicks up a shiny bronze lighter and lights her smoke.

That's another thing. Just like Klara and Jackson, these criminals have a great affection for smoking. Maybe that's just a 40's thing? Either way, makes me want to stay away from smoking even more now. I don't want to turn into jerks like them.

We have the majority of the components, the bits and pieces ready to be combined.

"Pass me the torch, Jon."

"Sure," I say as I hand Chuck the welder. Chuck fires it up and begins to heat the pieces of the would-be device.

"Chuck," I say over the sound of the flame, "this is like our best weapon right here, man. I know the flame doesn't shoot very far but it could definitely do some damage. You got any ideas?"

"Yeah, I was thinking the same thing." Chuck confirms.

Vasily overhears us and steps a bit closer passing us another piece of metal to weld.

"That's a great idea!" Vasily says, with an excited yet still whispered, expression. "But what do we do?"

"I brought a freeze ray too, so maybe that can help a bit?"

"Wait? You guys have a freeze ray?" asks

Vasily, as he hands Chuck yet another part.

"Yup, sure do."

"That's great! How powerful is it?"

"Oh, it's powerful enough. Deadly powerful!" I explain.

"Good! We'll use that to our advantage. I just don't know how yet."

"Well, no worries, whatever we end up doing we still have to finish building this thing."

Chuck pulls his welding mask down over his face and begins to make another crude addition to the new temporal device. I reach over Vasily and take a look at the blueprints to check on our progress. I can't fool myself into thinking that I understand the slightest bit of these blueprints, but it does look like we are making some much-needed headway towards a completed product. And no time is too soon.

Abby and Pete are still back with Russian Valentina and her two toadies. I am not worried about Abby; she can take care of herself. I am sad, however, that, once again, she has a gun aimed at her and is being held against her will. So much for time travel adventures like the movies and the books we're accustomed to. She's the one who keeps me and Pete out of trouble, but, unfortunately for her, we seem to be getting her into more and more trouble each trip.

I am more worried about Pete's brazen, act-now-think-later mindset. I just don't want him to do or say anything stupid, something that we will all regret. I love him like a brother even though he is just a cousin, but sometimes, he definitely acts on his emotions when his temper flares. Abby does too, but usually, the outcome is a bit better.

I take a glance at Pete over my shoulder and see the expression on his face. He's pissed and it shows. A blush of red washes over his face as beads of sweat begin to appear on his forehead. I know he feels helpless, as we all do, but more so because Abby is right there with him. I know they dig each other but are just too stubborn to admit it. Hopefully, he won't do anything stupid and act like a hero to impress her. I wish there was some way to let him know that we are working on an exit plan.

Turning around, I take another look at the blueprints and compare our progress to the product. Chuck and Vasily feverishly work in tandem to piece the device together bit by bit. I know Vasily had perfected the glitch before, but now, being under all this pressure, I will be happy if it works at all.

"No, Chuck! Look! Look at this piece here!" says Vasily, as he grabs the blueprints from me.

"Look, this equation here at the bottom. It's all wrong! I mean, it can't be right!"

"Okay, so fix it," says Chuck, matter-of-factly.

"I know! I know! I . . . I think it's gotta be . . . here! Vasily takes a pencil from his back pocket and enthusiastically begins to write out an entirely new equation on the blue prints. He writes a complete equation, erases it, writes a new one, erases it, and then finally settles on his third attempt.

"This is it! It has to be! This is why it was acting so funny all of the time," he says as he turns around and faces me.

"Your original device, the one you used to come back here, the thermal switch was using a pulsating equilibrium! Every time you used it, it faced a retrograde and ate away at the core! I just had to adjust the velocity equation and, there it is! That should do it!" Vasily smiles at Chuck who nods, turns back at me and gives a thumbs up. Not having any clue at what Vasily said, I give a simple nod, smile and two thumbs up.

"Hand me the torch and another thing of solder," Vasily commands as he lowers his mask once again.

"Hurry up you two!" Valentina says while jabbing Pete's back with her gun. Her thugs' menacing eyes pierce mine as my lip curls in disgust.

"Actually, I think just a few more pieces and it'll be done. I mean, granted it's kind of crude and a bit bulkier than the original, but I think at its core, it's better built, stronger and longer-lasting," says Vasily.

"Good! It had better be! All in the name of Mother Russia!" Valentina shouts from the back of the room.

"Mother Russia . . . Mother Russia . . ."

"It's okay, man. We'll work something out!" Chuck reassuringly says to Vasily. He regains focus and turns back to his work.

"One more clamp, one more bolt and that's it!" Vasily says, holding the device in the air.

"Yes!" says Chuck.

"Yes, indeed!" say Valentina as she walks towards us and grabs the device from Vasily's hands."

"HEY!" I yell.

"Hey, nothing!" she retorts. "Olaf. Yuri. Bring them up here."

Olaf nods his head and points to us. Pete and Abby follow his ogre-like command and slowly make their way over.

Just then the door to the lab is broken open followed up with a "Hold it right there!" It's Henry, the guard, followed by four of Chicago's finest, brandishing their firearms aimed at Valentina and her two grunts.

CHAPTER FIFTEEN

Valentina's henchmen reveal that they are also armed. They unholster their guns and open fire on Henry and the officers.

Valentina drops the new time device and takes aim as well. That motion seems to be Pete's cue to take action. He runs up behind her and grabs the device from the ground while whispering, "Yoink!"

The five of us take off running in the opposite direction of the firefight.

"Come on!" I yell to Abby and Pete, as Chuck and Vasily lead the way, the same path we took when we exited before.

The officers, two uniformed, two plain clothes, return fire and take refuge behind Henry's recently overturned guard desk. Their three opponents do the same and shield themselves behind Chuck's lab desk and workspace. One of the officers shoots Olaf. It strikes him and gets lodged in his left shoulder. The Russian behemoth doesn't flinch but instead lets out a faint grunt and continues firing, only this time with more anger in his eyes.

At first, we remain unnoticed what with all the gunfire. We're almost out of the room when

Valentina turns around to reach for the device.

Noticing that it's missing, she further turns and spots us at the tail end of our departure.

"STOP THEM!" she screams at the top of her lungs, causing Pete to lose a step and trip over a misplaced chair. He crashes to the floor. I stop, turn back, reach out my hand and pull him up as fast as I can. He quickly regains his footing as we finally exit the room.

"Quick! This way!" Vasily commands as we follow him down the darkened hallway. We reach the end and find another officer waving us towards him. He is tall, skinny and black, which comes as a surprise since this is the 40's; even the military is still segregated.

We turn left, all the while still running away from the crazy Russian and her crew. "Get behind me!" the officer yells. We take shelter behind the young officer as he cautiously looks down the hall.

"They're right behind us!" Abby explains.

"Who is? I was just outside walking the beat and picked up the call from the police box at the corner. I heard the shots fired and came as soon as I could!" says the officer.

"The Soviets are after us!"

"Soviets? Here in America? But wait, we're fighting against the Nazis! The Soviets are on our side. Right?" the officer asks, cautiously.

"Hold that thought," I say, "Here they come!" Valentina and her thugs come bounding out of the doorway, pause, take a look left and right, hear the commotion and head our way. The cop draws his gun as they slow their jog to a walk.

"Stop! In the name of the law!" yells the young cop with his weapon drawn.

"Well, whatdaya know about that?" she says. "A black police man. I tell you, you see everything in America!" She raises her gun and just as she is about to fire, the other cops catch up to them from the other side of the laboratory.

The officer doesn't waste any time and begins to unload his pistol on them. Seeking safety and shelter, the three Russians quickly break down a door across the hall and dodge the bullets. Valentina almost doesn't make it in, but Olaf shoves her and slams the door shut.

"Stay here!" says the cop as he motions with his hands towards the floor. He slowly creeps down the hallway up to the door and is met by Henry and the other four officers. Abby, Pete, Chuck, Vasily and I sit here, frozen, as if the freeze ray had stunned us into a mannequin position.

"On three! One! Two! Three!" yells one of the older cops as he kicks open the door with his right foot. The other officers pile into the room with guns ready. Then. Silence. We hear no gun fire, no struggle, nothing at all.

"What happened?" asks Abby.

"Dunno." I say.

The young black cop comes out, looks left

129

and right down the hall and then holsters his gun.

"It's okay now, kids. You can come out now. It's safe!"

"What happened?" asks Chuck.

"Did you get them?" questions Abby. The cop shakes his head back and forth and says, "The window is open. Looks like they headed down the fire escape. Sorry guys. Now I just need to take a statement from you guys to help me fill out these reports, okay?" He retrieves a pen and notepad from his left pants pocket.

"Statements?" I whisper to Chuck. "We don't have time for this. They are still out there and will be looking for us."

"Officer Johnson!" calls a voice from inside the other room.

"Coming, Sergeant," he replies. "He probably wants me to run out to the nearest call box and put out and all-points-bulletin. Me being the rookie, I get all the fun jobs. Okay, I'll be right back. Just find a seat or something, guys." Officer Johnson says as he heads back into the room.

"Let's go! Now's our chance!" I say.

We quickly, but quietly, scurry down the hall in our original direction. I look back to make sure the officers are still occupied. I also make sure we are still in possession of the newly-crafted temporal device. Everything looks good.

We continue to run down the hall, and finally see daylight peaking out of a window next to a short set of five steps. Sure enough the steps lead us to another main doorway that leads out to the street.

"Okay, what now?" Abby asks. "We can't go back to the dorms."

"Yeah, that's too obvious." I add.

"Well, where then?" Abby says while looking at Vasily and Chuck, together.

"Don't look at me! I'm all out of options. We could go to some other dorm or something?" Chuck offers.

"I know where you can go!"

"Look out!" Pete screams.

Valentina, still brandishing her gun, pops out from behind the shadow of a city bus. She grabs Vasily and shoves her gun in his back. A quickly approaching four door, green sedan comes screeching to a halt. The front right tire pops up over the curb. Olaf is behind the wheel seated next to Yuri. I guess they never took driving lessons while in the states.

"Everyone get in! Take seat! Take seat!" Olaf commands.

We reluctantly get into the car. We really have no other choice with a gun pointed at us. I mean, if I have to, I guess I could always blast her with the freeze ray and immobilize her Russian ass. But since she is the one with a real gun and Olaf is backing her up, barking orders, there is no time to act right now. I don't want to accidently blast Vasily into a billion tiny pieces.

We cram into the sedan, all eight of us, and

surprisingly all fit. Good thing this is the 40's or one of us would be strapped onto the roof and someone else stuffed into the trunk. Needless to say, this car is enormous.

Olaf peels out, throwing us off the curb and onto the pavement, heading away from the building. We gradually make our way off the side street and onto a main thoroughfare. The downtown Chicago skyline is in the distance as the midday sun casts shadows of both old and new skyscrapers.

As we continue to draw closer to the city, Olaf keeps the driving easy. Valentina remains silent, save an occasional sneer as she peers through the windshield. She is probably fantasizing about being promoted and rising in the ranks of the Soviet government. It would be a sure shot, too, taking our device and claiming it as her own.

I take a glance at the driver side mirror and see a silver car coming up behind us. I swear it's the same one I saw across the street when we were leaving the building. Not many silver cars around here, so this one definitely stands out.

I nudge Chuck who is seated to my left. He checks out the mirror but shrugs his shoulders. Knowing how much of a car guy he is, I give Pete a quick kick in the leg.

"That's a Mercedes-Benz 770 F-Cabriolet!" shouts Pete, as I kick him again, only harder.

"Quiet down back there! We will be at location soon, very soon." Valentina barks.

"Dude! Sorry, Jon, but what about that car? I mean, besides the fact that it's bad-ass."

"Just whisper, Pete. I am pretty sure it's following us."

"You think it's the cops," asks Vasily.

"What?! No way, not in a car like that. But just keep watch."

Our car continues for another two miles or so until Olaf takes a right exit that leads us to a city street.

"Look! You were right, Jon!" says Pete.

"Cool it, man. We don't know anything yet." And don't let on that we're being followed either. This could be our only way out!" I explain.

"Okay, but look, we just made another right turn and they are still tailing us," says Pete.

"Yeah, it's definitely following us now." It's not too hard to tell either. That's the most conspicuous car ever. "Now we just need to figure out who it is and who would have a ritzy car like that."

"I don't know, Jon, but I think we're about to find out. Brace yourself!"

The Mercedes is like a ship from the Roman Empire approaching ramming speed. If that's what they're really planning, they must not care too much about their car or money in general for that matter.

The jig is up. Olaf sees the beautiful machine in his rearview mirror and responds by flooring the gas pedal.

"What is it?" Valentina asks as she looks over to Olaf. He responds by nodding his head towards the mirror. "We have company," he says.

Valentina turns in her seat and gives an evil death stare to the driver of the Mercedes who continues to gain on us. At this point I'm not sure if I want it to catch up to us or not. They could be better than Valentina and her thugs. Then again, they could be worse. Which is the lesser of two evils? I dunno, but with a car like that, I'll take my chances.

With that thought in mind, I turn around and wave my hands and arms wildly. The others follow suit and start flailing their arms as much as possible.

"Stop that right now! Who is this? Who is this in this car?"

"I dunno lady, but sure beats you!" says Abby.

Valentina's face gets as red as Rudolph's nose as she pounds on Olaf's right shoulder to make him go faster. To that, he only responds, "I going, I going!"

He pulls a sharp right turn which throws us all to the left side of the car, making a human sandwich. Our tires screech as the rear end drifts to the left and back to the right as Olaf corrects our course.

The Benz is still on our tail. The only thing that comes between our cars is a metal trash can that Olaf clips on the side of the street.

The huge front end of the luxury car gets

134

closer and closer.

"Oh! Oh! Hey, guys, I know who that is!" Vasily says right before the Benz makes a second approach. The car gets too close for comfort and at our speeds of around 60 mph on the side streets of Chicago, it's pretty dangerous. The front right portion of the long silver hood gently nudges our rear left fender and we are forced into a spin to the left and then back around again in 360 degrees of screeching tires. I think he just performed the first P.I.T. maneuver on us!

We come to a stop, our rear end hangs out in the lane of oncoming traffic. The Mercedes now blocks our way out.

Not too dazed or confused, but definitely defeated, Olaf and the others quickly exit the car with guns ready. They are met by four men already outside of the Benz. They are sporting decked-out suits, topped with fedoras, which must have cost a fortune. Each of them brandishes what appear to be Tommy guns. I only have one guess here . . . it's the mob!

CHAPTER SIXTEEN

Well, I should have expected as much. I try my best to avoid stereotypes, but we *are* in Chicago and even though we're past the age of prohibition and Al Capone, it looks like *la Cosa Nostra* is alive and well.

But what do they want? Could they know about the temporal device? Vasily said he knew them. Was the mob working with the Soviets?

One man, still in the car, stands out from the rest. He's in a different suit: light blue, double-breasted with dark pinstripes. He has an enormous ruby ring on his left ring finger, and gold-framed sunglasses. He steps out of the back of the car, and says, "Let Oliver and his friends out of the car and we'll call it a day."

A sigh of relief comes over me as these guys, mob or not, appear to be on our side.

"Hey. Who's that guy?" I ask Vasily.

"It looks like . . . yeah, I was right! That's my, my girlfriend's father!"

"Whaaa?" I say.

"Yeah! Man, I knew she said her dad was really vested in his work, but this is ridiculous! He really does look like a mob boss! I had no idea!!!"

"My name is Vincent Dellepio. And, once again, I'm tellin' you to release those kids. NOW! Capisce?" exclaims the apparent mob boss while he reveals his own piece hidden under his suit coat.

"Yes, I heard you. I heard you just fine," Valentina says as she tells us to slowly get out of the car.

"Whoa, wait a minute, do I detect a little Russian accent, there?" says Vincent.

"Russian, no, whatever do you mean? I am from . . . Minnessotta," Valentina says, reverting back to her fake American accent.

"Here. Here you go. There is Oliver and friends. Sorry for the misunderstanding. We just wanted to have a little chat, that's all. A chat."

"Hey, Ollie. You and your friends alright?" asks Vincent, while stepping a few feet closer to our car.

"Yes. Yes, sir, Mr. Dellepio. Thank you, sir," replies Vasily.

"Still coming over this weekend for Mrs. Dellepio's famous spaghetti and meatballs?"

"Yes, sir. Barbara would kill me otherwise!"

"I will kill you, that is for sure!" Valentina says under her breath.

"What was that?" asks Dellepio.

I hold my breath. I have never been in a situation like this before, but this is a prime example of the phrase, 'so quiet you could hear a pin drop.'

"Come on over here guys. Let's let your friends go on their way. I'll give you a lift. Where yous guys headed?"

As we slowly walk to Vincent and his crew, two black coupes creep up on a side street parallel to us. The cars have all their windows rolled down and are packed with guys.

"Vinnie," cries the driver of the Mercedes, "It's the Fugazzio family!"

"No way!" says Chuck. "Those two mob families are arch rivals! Hit the deck!"

As if on cue, the two black coupes come to a stop. The occupants draw their Tommy guns and begin to open fire from inside their vehicles. The bullets rip through the rear and side windows of the Mercedes. The Dellepio crew kneel down behind the open car doors and return fire. It's one guy behind each door. Vincent seeks shelter in front of the massive grill of his once majestic, but now bullet-riddled car. His men quickly return fire but their opponents are relentless. They continue to unload their guns without hesitation.

Valentina and her thugs, on the other hand, pile back into their car. They tear off straight ahead, their only way out, and go flying down the street. We are stuck to fend for ourselves.

We get off of the street and huddle together under a green and white striped awning that marks the entrance of a pizza place. I reach up and pull on the brass handle of the glass door, but it won't budge.

Pete lends a hand and yanks on the handle as Abby tightly holds onto him. I look over at the window to the right of the door and notice a sign that reads:

CLOSED FOR RENOVATIONS

"Watch out!" says Chuck as he turns over a skinny ash tray/trashcan combo. Old cigarette butts, sand and trash pour over the sidewalk. Chuck takes hold of the receptacle with both hands, brings his arms back and slams the trashcan into the door of the pizza place.

Not pausing a moment to let Chuck wipe the rest of the glass shards from the door frame, Abby shoves her way through and enters the shop. We follow her lead and make it in safely on our hands and knees.

I look around as we stand and begin to dust ourselves off. We huff and puff as we check each other out. Everything looks good; there are no bullet wounds for us, just a couple cuts and scrapes from crawling on the broken glass. Anything is better than getting shot and we have avoided it thus far.

Outside, bullets continue to fly everywhere, some striking the car, but most missing their targets as the men aren't really aiming and are instead spraying the whole area. A few bullets ricochet across the street. One of Vincent's men gets shot in the lower leg, the only part of his body unshielded by the massive car doors. He falls to his feet and then collapses on his side, clenching his leg in pain.

Another one of the men, the guy behind him, using the front right door as a shield, tightly hugs the road and drags the wounded guy to the front of the car with Vincent.

At that, seeing that they have done at least *some* damage, the two coupes speed off.

"Quick, Jimmy," orders Vincent, "Throw him in the back seat and head over to the hotel. We gotta get his leg stitched up! Call Dr. Leo Verrozo at St. Francis Hospital. He owes me a favor."

"Sure, boss."

"Then, I want you guys to get ten other men and get revenge on those sonsabitch Fugazzios!!!"

"No problem at all, boss!"

"Hey!" says Vincent. "Where'd the kids go?" Vincent looks around until he hears the crunch of broken glass under our feet.

"Hey, you kids okay in there?" Vincent asks as he steps on some of the broken glass while approaching the pizza parlor.

"Yes, sir. We are all fine, thanks!" says Vasily.

"Okay, good. Well, just stay away from those other crumb-bums, alright? Something wasn't right with those guys. Anyways, I gotta run. Gotta take care of some unfinished business," he says as he adjusts his collar. "Check on you later, alright, Oliver?"

"Yes, sir. Tell Babs I said hello."

"Will do, kid. Will do."

The driver of the Benz throws his gun into the car and helps Vincent dust off his suit.

They finish piling in and take off in the damaged, yet still classy, automobile.

"Whoa, guys! That was so bad-ass! We totally just saw a real life mobster shootout!" says Pete, who picks up a barstool and pretends to fire it like a Tommy gun.

"Yeah, but this was real, Pete!" says Chuck as he puts his hands on Pete's shoulders. "You think you would understand that by now."

"I know, I know. But it was still awesome!" Pete admits.

"So, what now?" asks Vasily.

"We just gotta make sure we lay low," says Chuck as he opens an old ice box, in search of a cold beverage.

"Yeah, and speaking of laying low, wow Vasily! Leave it up to an undercover Russian scientist to get involved with the daughter of a mob boss," Abby says while smiling and shaking her head.

"Well, shoot, I really had no clue until all of this happened. I mean, I had my suspicions. Although, it does kind of make sense now that I think about it."

"What do you mean?" Abby asks.

"Well, their family seemed to have an awful amount of money for owning a milk delivery

141

company: rings, watches, necklaces, the finest suits, not to mention that car!"

"Yeah, not to mention the big cross-stitched plaque hanging over their fireplace that says, I heart the mob. Ha-ha!" says Pete, once again, amused by his own joke. He looks around and realizes he is the only one laughing and says, "Aw, you guys suck!"

"So, what now?" Abby asks on a serious note.

"I dunno. Where do, do . . . do you . . ."

"Chuck, what are you talking about man?" I ask. "Chuck?" I look over at Chuck and find him stumbling to and fro. "You okay, dude?" I ask.

"Yeah, I just . . ." he says as he begins to fall forward. He goes head first into a red and white checkered booth and takes a fake fern with him on the way down.

"Chuck!" cries, Abby.

We rush over to help him up but it's no use. He's out cold. I lift up his left arm and feel his wrist for a pulse. But, once again, nothing. I press two fingers on his neck and finally get a faint beat.

"Jon, look! His neck!" notes Pete.

I pull his collar down slightly as it reveals the tip of a dart.

"It's another tranquilizer! Everybody, eyes open! Take cover!" I command.

"No need for that," says the recognizable femme fatale. Valentina and Olaf have returned and Yuri is probably not too far behind.

142

CHAPTER SEVENTEEN

"Nice shot," says Vasily.

"Thank you, my boy. But to be quite honest, I was aiming for you. Oh, well. I was quite far away. But never mind that."

Valentina removes another gun from her hip and takes aim at a beer mug on the bar at the other end of the parlor. She fires and shatters the mug all over the bar top.

"Be assured, I will not miss my target again. Olaf, take him to the car. The rest of you follow! And no funny business! This time you will not be saved by your little American mobsters."

As we slowly and reluctantly exit the pizza parlor, I realize that she is right; there's no sign of Vincent and his crew. They are probably long gone, on their way to get revenge on that other mob family. No superhero mobsters to come rescue us this time. I find it ironic that I am praying for the mob, of all people, to save us.

We once again crunch the shards of broken glass on the ground as we reclaim our seats in their car. Yuri flings Chuck onto Pete's lap. He is still out cold. It could be worse. She could have just straight up shot him. They shut the doors and Olaf starts the engine.

"Where to?" Olaf asks.

"We will head back to the dorms. That will be best bet," says Valentina.

"Good. Very good," says Olaf as he starts to drive us back to campus. Yuri pulls his shoulder and tucks it back in order to look at us and says, "So you boys and girls have created some sort of time machine, huh?" He then mumbles something Russian to Valentina and looks at us again.

"Well, please tell me about this device."

We don't say a word.

"Answer him!" orders Valentina.

"Yes, please tell us everything. We need to know how to use this thing," says Yuri.

We remain silent until Yuri pulls his sidearm and presses it hard against Chuck's back. Out of options, I ask, "Well, what do you wanna know?"

"Everything, of course. From the begining."

"Well, we didn't build it, not the original anyway; that came from the Russkies' good old friends, the Nazis."

"The Nazis! No! Never!" Olaf says as he pounds his enormous fist on the dashboard. "First off we are not friends. Stalin should have never trusted that bastard Hitler by signing The Non-Aggression Pact. That was such bad mistake. Well, that was not so bad, but his double crossing us with Operation

144

Barbarossa! They will pay for this dearly! Mother Russia will not let that fascist terrorize our country!"

"Well, that's nice I suppose. But, yeah, a Nazi scientist is behind the original blueprints."

"There is no way those bastards could discover, let alone *invent* time travel! This is absurd! What makes you say this to me?!"

"Uhhhh, the truth, perhaps?" says Abby, matter-of-factly.

"It is the truth, Olaf," says Chuck , coming out of his tranquilizer stupor and speaking hesitantly to ensure that Yuri doesn't accidentally pull the trigger.

"Welcome back, Chuck!" says Pete. Chuck nods and sits up as much as possible and says, "It was hard for me to believe, too, Olaf. But it's the truth."

"What? Never? Give story. Give quickly!"

I swear the more agitated and frustrated Olaf becomes, the more his English sounds like that of a caveman.

"Alright," says Chuck. "The quick story is, the granddaughter of a Nazi scientist attempted to use it for her own means to go back in time and save her grandfather's life."

"Then is true!"

"Wow," Pete whispers to me, "He didn't need much convincing. We could have told him anything!"

"Ha, yeah." I reply.

145

Funny thing is Pete's probably right. Well, he wanted the short story and that's it. I'm kinda glad Chuck didn't divulge too much information, unnecessarily.

We continue to make our way back to Chuck and Vasily's dormitory, exiting the highway and reentering the University of Chicago campus. Olaf purposefully takes us by the research facility to get an idea of the police activity. We don't drive right by it, but instead, take a cross street, and stop at an intersection.

A block away, we can see the research facility is still jumping. There are about seven police cars, twenty or so cops, a few reporters and several dozen onlookers. One little boy, about ten years old, jumps up and down behind the police barricade to try to get a closer look.

"Good, they are still occupied at the research facility. We simply head back to dormitory and get this thing up and running," says Valentina.

"Yeah, but the cops will go there to look for us! That security guard, Henry, he knows Chuck and Vasily. All the cops have to do is find out where their dorm is," says Pete with a look of confidence.

"This is true!" says Olaf.

"Okay. I have another place in mind, then. Thank you, Peter is it? Good Russian name, you know?" says Valentina with a smirk.

"Great job, Peterrrrr! Our only chance to get rescued and you blow it! That *is* a great Russian name isn't it? Well whose side are you on anyway?" Abby yells as she punches Pete in the shoulder as hard as she can in our confined, restricted seats.

"Ouch! I'm sorry, okay. I was just sayin' is all! Geez!" Pete says as he lifts up his sleeve and begins to rub his shoulder. "That's gonna bruise, too."

"Well, good! I wanted it to hurt. Just remember to think before you speak, Pete, or, at least, run it by Jon or me before you flap those lips!"

"Abby! Chill! I think he's gotten the point!" I say.

"Yes, yes, you two love birds back there shut up, alright? I need it quiet so we can find new destination."

"Lovebirds? She wishes," says Pete with a look of disgust on his face.

"Ha-ha," Valentina says, "We shall see!"

We drive past the dorms and sure enough, big-mouth Pete was right. It was also swarming with cops, not as many as at the lab, but still too many for us to get inside unnoticed.

As we continue to drive by the dorms, Officer Johnson, the one who shielded us from the gunfire back at the research facility, glances over at us. He pauses a minute and then, as if it just clicked, he takes a double take at Olaf.

"There they are!" he yells to his commanding officer as we clear the dormitory.

The sedan rumbles and lets out a puff of grey smoke as Olaf steps on the gas.

"Damn it!" says Valentina. "Why did you take us this way? You imbecile! The stupid boy even warned us!"

Olaf looks over at Valentina with a sneer on his face.

"Go! Go! Go!" Yuri shouts as the cops hop into their squad cars and begin pursuit.

"You tell me nothing, Valentina! Where you like me to go?"

"Anywhere now, you idiot! Just drive us anywhere away from here!"

"You know what?" Olaf says as he receives a nod from Yuri. "I tell YOU where to go, Valentina. You go to hell!" Olaf unexpectedly slams on the breaks which allows the police to easily catch up to us.

"What are you doing? What did I just tell you! Drive you big bafoon! Drive!"

Yuri opens his car door and exits. With both hands, he reaches inside and pulls Valentina, kicking and screaming, out of the car. He holds her in the air by her waist as she screams, "Put me down! Put me down! What are you doing!" She continues to kick and hit him which doesn't affect him at all. He finally lets go and she falls on her butt. Bothered and bewildered, she looks up at Yuri, while huffing and puffing.

Yuri stares her down and steps towards her once

again.

"No! Stay away from me!" she says as she starts to back pedal on all fours as if she were in a cheesy horror movie trying to flee an assailant. He reaches down towards her waist pocket and says, "You won't need this anymore." He relieves her of the temporal device. She grabs hold of it, but quickly loses grasp of the cylinder when Yuri offers a quick tug. Defeated, she falls back to the ground.

"Come now, Valentina. You really think that you, a simple woman, would be able to rise through the ranks of the Soviet Union? I doubt things change that much in just few years. Future leaders would never listen to you. No way. Me and Olaf have no problem ending up on top with this one."

"Are you kidding me? I thought we were team!" she retorts.

"Yeah, well this time, on this team, I call the shots."

"Put your hands up!" shouts the first arriving police officer. The other cops park their cars, exit and take aim while resting their arms on the tops of the car doors.

"Here! She is all yours!" Yuri says, as he spits at her feet. He runs back in the car, shuts the door and we take off once again. I think we were all so shocked and it happened so quickly that we didn't realize we could have taken that opportunity to jump out of the car. Who would have thought Valentina's two big thugs would double cross her? Well, as they say, you can never trust a criminal, even if you are one yourself.

I turn around and look over my shoulder to see the rookie officer retrieving and handcuffing Valentina. She simply sits there, paralyzed by shock, and stares at us as we drive away.

"Okay, guys, sooooo . . . you're gonna let us go now, right? This stop is ours or right here at the next corner will be fine," says Abby. I don't think she honestly believes they'll let us out, but just figures she would give it a try nonetheless.

"No, we carry on with plan, only this time, we are in charge, not that obnoxious hag. We do all her dirty work no longer. No longer she barks orders at us all day and all night!"

"Oh, um, okay," says Abby. "So carrying on with the plan, ay? Well, where are you taking us then?"

"We *take* nowhere. We *go* somewhere instead; we use time device while driving. Is as simple as that."

Maybe we underestimated the intelligence of Valentina's muscle. Use the time machine while in the car? Why not? It worked in *Back to the Future*, right? You never know. Maybe the whole car will go back with us.

"Hey, Vasily, with this new and improved device, will that actually work? I mean, could it work that way? Would the car go back with us or would it just remain driving, driverless and crash into something?"

"Actually, I made it so either is possible."

"Whoa, really?" I ask.

"Yeah, it wasn't that hard. Just a simple modification in one equation."

"Nice!"

"Yes, why don't you tell us all about device now. I think would be good idea to bring car, don't you? That way we won't have to steal car of fellow Russian," says Olaf.

"Ummm, not too sure about that. We probably won't be arriving on a road and even so, if the car plops down on a road out of nowhere, we will definitely raise some eyebrows," comments Vasily.

"That's true," I add. "We would especially be noticed in an American car from the 40's."

"Hmmm, maybe you are right. Okay. So, before cops catch up to us, what do we enter here in row of flashing numbers?"

"Well, you need to enter the coordinates for where you want to go. So, um, where are we going actually?" I question.

"Like we said, we follow through with plan, but we take credit. Right, Yuri?!" Yuri chuckles, smiles and nods his head.

Vasily explains the particulars of the new machine to Olaf, Yuri and the rest of us. It's pretty much the same thing as the old one with a few modifications.

He fixed the thermal switch and told us that

151

we no longer have to worry about searching for the device when we reach our destination. If we are holding on to it, it will remain in our hands upon our arrival. He also fixed the power source and, believe it or not, made it able to be charged in any 20th century electric outlet. That really helps us now, but if we ever have to go deeper into the past . . . well, let's just hope this is our last time-travel excursion for a while!

Vasily explains how to enter the coordinates and while doing so, Abby whispers to me, "So, what are we gonna do? Any plan?"

"Not yet." I tell her. "We just gotta be on our guard, ready to move at any minute. Ya know?"

"Yeah, I got ya, Jon."

"Okay!" says Yuri, "No more time to waste! Next stop: 1960's Kremlin!"

And in an instant, we are giving the new device its first test run.

CHAPTER EIGHTEEN

All the same feelings are there again, the heat and cold fluxuations, but this time they are not nearly as extreme. And this time, unlike before, I can clearly see everyone around me while we're travelling through time.

I turn my head left and right and see the others. My movements are extremely slow. It reminds me of the sunken treasure game we used to play in the town pool. One person would throw some items and let them sink and the others took turns diving for them. Turning your head under water is slightly more strenuous than turning your head above water. And that's what it feels like now.

I attempt to talk to Pete and Chuck but they cannot hear me. Not because it's too loud, because it is really quite peaceful this time, but maybe it's because we're in a vacuum. Or . . . who knows? Maybe the laws of physics don't allow us to talk when we're not set in one specific time.

The car is still here with us, but it's blurry, like everything on the outside. Well, not really blurry, but more like when you take a photo of Christmas

153

lights and accidently move the camera, ever so slightly; the lights zigzag all over the place.

That reminds me of Dad when he tries to snap a perfect shot, saying, "I don't need the tripod. I have the fingers of a precision musician, the dexterity of a surgeon and the cunning of a magician!" And, of course, after each snap of the camera, the zigzag of lights steals the show and takes up the bulk of the photograph.

It's finally over. Wow! What an improvement. We're not scattered around all over the place like yesterday's dirty laundry, we don't have to search for the device because Yuri still has it in his hand and I dunno about everyone else, but I feel fine: no headache, neck ache, bumps, bruises, nothing at all! The only sensation I feel is cold and icy, but then again, we are sitting on a pile of snow.

"Vasily! Chuck! You guys rock! These improvements are awesome!"

"Huh?" they both respond in unison.

"He means this is the bee's knees!" says Pete, giving me the thumbs up.

"Oh, okay. Good. I'm glad. Although, I'm not sure I want to know what it was like before. I mean, geez. I am freezing cold and my ass is wet!" notes Chuck.

"Welcome to Russia," says Yuri with a disgusting grin as he stands and begins to pat the snow and ice from his pants. Olaf does the same only after staring at the device in awe of its power.

Pete helps Abby as the rest of us get to our feet.

"I'm fine. I'm fine. Get away!" says Abby as she refuses to take Pete's outstretched arm.

Pete, looking dumbfounded, says, "Fine!" and instead walks closer towards me.

Adjusted to the more stable and comfortable form of time travel with the new device, I look around and take in the scenery.

Even though we are in an area surrounded by shrubs and small trees, the traffic and fast paced life of a city is all around us. I push through a group of shrubs and sure enough, as planned, we are in Moscow; it's a very cold and snowy, nighttime Moscow at that.

The snow must have just recently ended because the streets are covered. Or maybe they just don't plow the streets here like they do back home, or back home in our time, I mean.

A horse drawn sleigh plows its way through the snow as a car follows the sleigh's path. Another car, in the oncoming lane, fishtails back and forth on the slippery snow and blows its horn at the horse as the car goes the wrong way. The horse driver takes the sleigh off the road and down a small hill and avoids a collision. The green car following the sleigh is not as lucky, however; the out-of-control car slams into the green car's front end. Both drivers get out and begin yelling at each other while pointing to their respective damage.

155

"Ahh, it is good to be back home!" says Olaf.

We begin walking to the Kremlin. Moscow, fully entrenched in Communism, still praises the glory of Lenin in this De-Stalinization era of the Soviet Union. A huge banner hangs on the side of a brick building. Its image depicts Lenin and his red followers in the background.

"Man, you guys sure have a funny writing. What's that say?" asks Peter confused by the letters of the Cyrillic alphabet.

"It says, '*I am the October Leader. Communists Forever*,'" says Vasily, as he shakes his head.

"Well, it's better than a mural of Stalin, I suppose." I say. Vasily smiles and nods his head in agreement.

We continue to walk on and spot another building dressed with Soviet propaganda. This time it's an enormous painting of Sputnik, the first man-made satellite, launched into space by the USSR in 1957. A mural of a cosmonaut is across from it.

"What's this one say?" asks Abby, as Olaf and Yuri keep increasing our pace by breathing down our necks and walking on our heels.

"*Gagarin – Glory of the party!*" says Vasily. "I am not sure who he is though. Maybe some future war hero? Funny helmet, see? And funny bomb next to him with little spikes"

"Oh, that's Sputnik. And he's the first man in space." I say.

156

Vasily stops and causes a chain reaction since he was in the lead.

"What stopping for?" asks Olaf.

"First man in space?" says Vasily. "That is amazing!"

"Ha-ha! Puny little Americans; so we put first man in space! That is great!!" says a very smug Yuri. "He must have gone up in little ball!"

"No. No. He wouldn't fit in Sputnik, dummy!" says Abby.

"Yeah, but don't get too happy about it. You guys started the space race, but we finished it! Good, old U S of A!" says a very complacent Pete, matter-of-factly.

"Oh, really? Well, how did you do that? Send up first woman?" asks Yuri.

"Ha-ha-ha!" they both laugh.

"Um. Well, no, actually. You guys did that first, too," Pete says, a little defeated, but then follows with, "We put a man on the moon, smart ass! So take that!"

"Man on moon?! No way! You are one delusional little boy! If you had man on moon, there is no way we would celebrate these Russian accomplishments so highly. They would be embarrassment to the Soviet people!"

"That's because it hasn't happened yet!" Abby clarifies.

"And it never will! Mother Russia will take over the USA and we will be the ones who land man on moon! Mark my words!" promises Olaf.

That keeps us quiet for awhile as we continue walking. A rusty old car without a muffler zooms by and splashes snow and ice all over Olaf.

"Ha!" Pete says, "Serves your right!"

"Shut up before I smash you to little pieces!" he says, huffing and puffing. "Besides, I would enjoy that much more than shooting you with pistol."

"Calm yourself, Olaf," says Yuri, "We have work to do!"

We continue walking and approach a more visible and highly illuminated part of the city, with fewer roads and more paved, yet snow covered paths and open spaces. Propaganda, however, is still very prevalent. A man in the center of the park passes out Communist pamphlets. Vasily and I take one but Olaf and Yuri prevent Pete, Chuck and Abby from getting one. They are obviously keeping their eyes on the prize and are trying to make sure we get there soon.

"What is it? What is it?" asks Pete.

"Yeah, Jon. What's it say?" asks Abby.

I give them the pamphlet but to their surprise, it's also in Cyrillic which means it's basically useless to them. Vasily opens his copy and begins to read aloud as we continue to trudge through the snowy park.

"It says, 'The Soviet Union stands strong against the OAS! An illegal blockade will not deter us from protecting our Communist brothers in Cuba!'"

158

"What's today's date?" I ask Olaf.

"Not sure. Valentina was one who entered numbers. Let me look." Olaf says as he takes the device out of his huge pocket, wipes the screen clean and reads, "October the 23rd, 1961."

"Then we are in the heat of it. The Cuban Missile Crisis is underway." I say.

"What this pamphlet mean by OAS? What is this OAS the pamphlet speaks of?" Yuri asks as he sticks me with his gun.

"That's the Organization of American States. It was formed after WWII for solidarity and cooperation between all of the American nations. It convened during the Cuban Missile Crisis. It was probably its most important meeting, to decide whether or not the nations would support the US on our quarantine of Cuba." I explain.

"What mean quarantine? Pamphlet say blockade?" asks Olaf.

"Well, we called it a quarantine to avoid any warlike implications. We also didn't want it to sound like Stalin's blockade of Berlin."

"Oh, I bet that is how we defeat the Nazis; we starve them into submission! I like it!"

"Wrong again!" says Pete in his game show announcer voice, "The answer we were looking for was 'first major event of the Cold War.' But we do have some wonderful parting gifts for you!"

Olaf continues walking with a scowl on his face, knowing that he has been made fun of,

159

but not knowing exactly how.

"He means that's not how we, yes, WE defeated the Nazis. After the war, Berlin was divided into four zones: French, British, American and Soviet. Eventually the three western zones joined together and Germany was cut in half between the West and East. The thing is, Berlin also got split up, even though it was completely surrounded by the Soviet sector. Stalin didn't want us to rebuild Germany and, instead, wanted to punish the German people. So he blocked access into Berlin for a little over a year." I further explain.

"That is good old Stalin for you, ha-ha!" Olaf jests, while jabbing Yuri in the side.

"We responded with the Berlin airlift and dropped thousands of pounds of food and supply."

"You know a lot of history, Jon. If we get out of this alive and you go back to your time, you should be a history teacher one day," comments Vasily.

"No way, man! Teaching would be so lame! I mean, why would anyone spend their whole childhood in school only to come back to it as an adult?"

We continue to walk and hold very tentative conversations, fully aware that the Soviet Union's 'finest' are ready to pull their triggers at a moment's notice. But what else can we do?

"Whoa! Guys, check that out," says Chuck as we cross another street. And there it is, the iconic onion topped and Easter-egg-colored St. Basil's Cathedral, towering above us.

I pause and think as it hits me. We are in Red Square, Moscow during the height of the Cold War. The Kremlin is just on the other side of the street. Some of the most historical decisions ever made have taken place there, perhaps even right now. Crazy thought. And one of those decisions is about to be influenced by Olaf and Yuri. Great.

Well, we can't let that happen. I don't know how, but we have to prevent the Russian takeover of the greater half of the US. We defeated Klara and Jackson and we can defeat these two clowns, too.

"Enough sight-seeing. Keep moving! Keep moving!" orders Olaf as he kicks my right heel.

CHAPTER NINETEEN

We finally reach the outer perimeter of the Kremlin. We huddle up around some bushes in yet another garden and await Olaf's next command.

"Okay, it looks like changing of the guard. We use this opportunity to sneak in." says Olaf.

"Sneak in?" questions Pete, "I thought you guys were high up on the Kremlin food chain. Can't we just walk right in?"

"No, sadly. Not yet. But we will be once we get face to face meeting with this, Khrushchev you speak of."

"Sounds like a great plan," says Abby, sarcastically. "So with all those Soviet soldiers and their guns, marching and kicking their feet high into the sky, we're gonna sneak in? No wonder you guys were just the hired muscle."

"How do you even know which building it is? There are over a dozen here!" says Chuck.

"Only one building is most important, the Great Kremlin Palace. That is where we will find our man, Khrushchev. Hey Yuri, you don't think this could be the same Khrushchev we used to know back in Vladvistok. Do you?"

"Little Khrushchev! No way he is in charge! Sure, he was always popular, but just no way!"

"Ha-ha! I guess you are right. Was just a thought! Hahahahaha!" They both slap each other's back and laugh as hard as they can. I have no idea how common the surname Khrushchev is, and right now, I don't really care. I am too preoccupied with worrying about getting shot, not only by the two stooges, but now by the Soviet troops that we're apparently about to bypass.

"Oh that is good one. Okay. Here is what we do."

Olaf explains the plan to Yuri and the rest of us. It doesn't seem like anything special at all; we are just going to sneak in while the troops are distracted by their strict routine.

I guess Olaf and Yuri don't realize we can simply use the device to transport ourselves inside. All we need are the coordinates. It would be a lot less risky. Crap. I can't find the freeze ray! I must have dropped it while running in the research facility. I sure could use that thing right now.

"Okay, ready?" Olaf motions for us to run, as he tucks his gun away and makes sure it's extra concealed. The Soviet guards begin the changeover march and pass the proverbially torch for the night.

"Now!" he orders as we all leap from behind the shrubs and creep towards the door, hunched over on our toes as quiet as we can.

163

And believe it or not, we make it to the cement wall that lies adjacent to the doorway, without being seen. There isn't the slightest hesitation from any of the guards at all. I'm sure it would have been more difficult if it were daytime with a gaggle of tourists viewing the changeover.

Olaf opens the massive door and we creep in as he quickly and quietly closes it behind us.

"Wow! This place is huge!" says Pete as he turns his head back and forth surveying the hallway.

"I can't believe security was so lax. Especially in the heat of the Cuban Missile Crisis!"

"I know. It's kinda too good to be true." I add.

And as always, as if on cue from a director waiting in the stage wings on opening night, about a dozen men, some in suits, others in military garb, come running towards us. We turn to try another route, but are surrounded in the t-shaped hallway as five more men join from the right. Four more come along from the left. They were probably watching us all along. Now I really hope Olaf and Yuri have a good plan.

The closest soldier starts barking out orders in Russian as Olaf replies.

"What are they saying, Vasily?" asks Pete.

"They want us to stop and put our hands on our heads. Olaf and Yuri are telling them they need to see Khrushchev and that it's of the greatest importance and pertains to the current crisis."

"Now what are they saying?" asks Pete.

"Now they are telling me to shut up and stop translating to you!"

"Oh, okay well you better stop then, Vasily!"

"Now he is telling *you* to shut up!"

"Oh. Well. Okay then." Pete says.

We take the warning and heed it with caution by keeping our mouths shut as we have a standoff with the troops. We are completely surrounded. They show no signs of giving us any breathing space or stretching room at all.

Olaf and Yuri are both frisked and their weapons are removed. A soldier mumbles something and Olaf and Yuri begin to show their credentials, which of course do not match up, being from the 40's. This fact begins to raise the suspicion of the troops which is expressed by their countenance.

One man takes a look at their dubious credentials, looks back at a subordinate who raises an eyebrow, and looks back at Olaf. Olaf, once again, begins to explain his case to the guards. Vasily translates in a whisper.

"These are old credentials. You are no longer permitted on these grounds and especially not with American children. What are you thinking?"

"No, I tell you, the picture, look at it. If that is true, I have not aged a bit. Look at his, as well. We are from the past, and they, they are from the future. We must speak to the Premier immediately for the sake of Mother Russia and future of the Soviet

Union!"

Olaf turns to Chuck and Vasily and says, "Hey, you two, I know you have one of those new driver cards they make you have in Illinois. Take them out and show them. Take out anything you have that will help us prove case or Gulag will send us all to Siberia!"

"He's right," I say as Chuck and Vasily dig through their wallets. I search through mine as well and pull out anything and everything I can find that would prove that we are not locals, locals to this decade or even this century.

I unfold my trifold and slide my finger under the cards behind the plastic display. I have last year's school ID, an old library card, a ticket stub from *Zombie Massacre 7* that Pete somehow talked me into seeing, a receipt from the comic book store and a scrap of paper with some math equations on it.   I separate the back section and thankfully have a five dollar bill. I look at the bottom right of the Abe Lincoln portrait and see the year reads 2011. Good enough!

Pete looks over and mouths the words, "I got nothing." Where did he spend all of his lawn mowing money? If I know Pete, it wasn't on anything necessary. Then again, if I had that kind of money, I wouldn't be saving much of it either.

"Give me! Give me!" says Olaf, as we hand him the contents of our wallets. He gives the items to the main soldier who begins thumbing through them.

The man looks at our information and seems particularly interested in my five dollar bill. He holds it up to the light, inspects the watermark and other unique features, and approaches me.

"So, you are from the future, huh?" he asks.

"Whoa, you speak English?" shouts Pete.

"Yes. I spent some time in the states. Long enough to know that this is not what the money looks like. At least, not now anyways."

"Well, could you please call off your men? I am really not happy with all these guns aimed at us," says Abby.

The man nods and calls out a brief Russian phrase which leads all the soldiers to lower their weapons.

"See! I told you! We have important news to tell the Premier! We must see him immediately!" says Olaf to the English speaking guard.

"Very good," the soldier says as he looks us over once again. He hands back our IDs, holds out my fiver and asks, "May I keep this?"

Like I'm gonna say no to this guy. "Of course!" I reply as he shoves it in his pocket. I don't think he was gonna give it back either way. Sucks for him. He won't be able to use it for another fifty years.

"Follow me," he says as his men file in line behind us.

We walk down the long corridor with extremely high ceilings, and reach an area that looks like the lobby of an upscale hotel, fully decorated

167

with classically-styled sofas adorned with gold-trimmed pillows with ornate details and stitching. The men disperse to different corners of the long room, of which we are told to stay in the center.

An enormous stuffed brown bear stands upright with his arms and claws extended well above his head. He is prominently placed in the center of the room under a huge hammer and sickle banner.

On the opposite side of the room is a huge display case, full of Faberge Eggs. I saw one on the *Antiques Roadshow* about a month ago and it was estimated to be worth twenty million dollars! This display case has about fifteen of them! The one in the center even has a clock on the front and a hinged top.

"I see you like my collection," a voice says from the doorway.

I turn around to see the main guard who spoke English to us. From behind him steps out none other than Nikita Khrushchev himself!

CHAPTER TWENTY

"Nikita! Is that really you?" asks Olaf.

"Olaf Lavrova?! Yuri Simonov?! Time has been good to you my friends! You haven't aged one bit!" Khrushchev says as he pushes his way through the guards and presents both hands to be shaken by Olaf and Yuri.

"It . . . It is you! Nikita, you are the Premier of the Soviet Union? I . . . I can't believe it!" Olaf says as he turns to Yuri with a confused expression; an expression that reminds me of Pete's when I try to teach him algebra.

"Ha! Why do you look so surprised? Surely you have known who your leader is for the past four years! Where have you been? Under a rock?" asks Khrushchev.

"No. No. Actually we, um . . ." The shock of seeing their old friend has not yet subsided from Olaf's mind. This is the same old friend they were just making fun of and laughing at the idea of him being in charge.

"No. We have not been under rock," Yuri

169

butts in, "And we have not aged since you knew us because, well, we have not yet lived in this time, in 19. . . uh, 19…" Yuri looks at me for help as I hesitantly mouth the words 'sixty two.'

"Yes, 1962. This is first time for us. You see, we are the Olaf and Yuri you knew from the 40's."

"Yes, yes," Khrushchev says, "I know that we have not seen each other since the 40's when you two were sent over to guard Valentina in America. You remember? She was keeping tabs on that little Russian genius of ours that was assisting with the American nuclear program."

"Yes! Vasily. He is right here with us!" Olaf points back at Vasily who tentatively and cautiously waves at Khrushchev.

"What? It . . . it cannot be! I mean, you are only around nineteen or twenty, how could this… what were you saying again about this being your first time in 1962?" Khrushchev asks, getting up close and personal with Olaf, only inches from his face as he stares into his eyes.

Dismayed, Khrushchev motions us to sit down. We head over to the heavily upholstered sofa and take a seat. This thing looks ancient, but I swear it feels better than our new couch back home.

The Premier asks for a more clear explanation of things: who we are, where we are from and why things seem, "not quite right," as he puts it. Yuri and Olaf have failed at this task so Chuck, Vasily and I take the reins and begin to explain the whole thing, bit by bit, piece by piece, detail by time-travelling detail. And finally, he gets it.

He is shocked of course. I suppose that's the proper response upon learning that time travel is not only possible, but you have living proof standing right in front of you.

Khrushchev stands up, rubs his head and sits down. He stands up again and walks around the room. Finally, he comes back to us, sits down and says, "So, why come here to me? Why now during this October crisis? Does something go terribly wrong? Who fires the first nuke! I bet you it is hot-headed Kennedy! What happens? Tell me! Tell me!"

"We win! We take over entire west coast of America using this little device!" claims Yuri as he presents the device to Khrushchev.

"That's not true!" yells Abby.

"That's not how it's supposed to be!" I add.

"You shut up! You have spoken too much already!" Olaf says as he shoots a threatening look our way.

"No, Olaf! You let them speak! They seem to know just a little bit more about all of this than you do!" Khrushchev orders as his guards once again display their guns. Olaf backs down and takes a more relaxed posture on the sofa.

"Now, children. Please. Continue," Khrushchev says.

"Well, what he said was right. I mean, it did happen, but it only happened because of me," Vasily

171

starts. "As it was explained to me, after I completed my time in America, I was sent back to Russia. I sought political asylum in America but was refused. I was very bitter towards the US. I made the device and showed you how it could be used. We had Castro launch some nuclear missiles out to sea as a distraction while we transported our forces to the West coast of America. The Americans were caught off guard as the majority of their forces were on the other coast near Cuba. But I was wrong in doing that. I mean, the future me, that is to say. I will not do that. I will not let my anger get the best of me. That is not what is supposed to happen."

"Well, what is supposed to happen? How does this all pan out for Russia and the Soviet Union?"

"I'll take this, Vasily." I say as Khrushchev focuses on me.

"Sir, what I am about to tell you is how it's supposed to happen. The way that we *all* win."

"Yes. Please. Go on."

I explain how it all goes down. I explain how it ends up and how it's written in history books. The correct way, where the Soviets remove the missiles and ship them back to Russia and we never invade Cuba again. The way when the Cold War rages on, but America is still comprised of the good old 50 states from sea to shining sea. I do, however, leave out the part about our missiles in Turkey. No need to complicate the matter further.

"Although, the Cuban Missile Crisis was a terrible and, simply put, scary time, I think it was necessary. It was necessary for the two superpowers to experience. We needed a major shakeup, a showdown between the two of us. The Korean War was over and we were not yet fully entrenched in Vietnam. The Cuban Missile Crisis was a wakeup call where cooler heads needed to and, thank God, prevailed. Both sides realized that showing off, that flexing some muscle was okay, so long as the muscle doesn't drive the decisions and launch death upon the world." I continue to explain.

"Although there were other events of the Cold War, the Cuban Missile Crisis helped warm it up a bit, just a little bit mind you. One thing was a direct hotline established between the . . . well, here, the Kremlin, and the Whitehouse." I finish up.

"Good, I am sick of teletype machine!" Krushev says as he rubs his chin.

"So, we have no problems after this? This will make us friends?"

"Well, not really. But with this event we learned to compromise. That was a great start. I won't tell you too much, but the Cold War will end, sir.

"Hmm. Good. So, diplomacy does work sometimes."

He continues to rub his chin and look towards the Faberge eggs. He goes over, opens the cabinet and takes out the Russian egg centerpiece that

173

previously drew my attention.

"This was the last tsar's favorite piece. Do you know the legacy and history of the Russian people? We are strong and wise. But, sometimes we are stubborn, too. If I want our legacy to last and remain for future generations of Russians and the entire world, I will do what is right. I can't believe I'm saying this. Maybe you caught me on a good day, but . . . I will follow the correct path, my friends. Once offer is made, I will abide by it and not screw things up." Khrushchev says with a smile.

"Thank you, sir!" We give a collective sigh of relief as the pressure is taken off our shoulders.

"Nikita! I know we have not always seen eye to eye, but trust me, you need to do this! You need to do this for Mother Russia! It will be biggest victory the world has ever seen!"

"Perhaps you are right, Olaf."

"Yes! Yes!" says Yuri.

"No! No!" says Abby.

Khrushchev turns to Abby and smiles.

"But at what cost, Olaf? At what cost? You kids remind me of my own kids when they were younger. And I would never, NEVER do anything to hurt them or their futures. And so," he says as he looks to the ground then back at us, "as I said, we will do it the way you say it goes, not with silly time machine, altering everything. Although I admit, it is pretty neat to know time travel is possible," he says while handing the device to Vasily.

174

"Good thing you came to me instead of Stalin or some of my other predecessors, ha-ha! They would have used this power not only to take over the United States, but the whole world as well!"

"Premier Khrushchev!" interrupts a man who runs into the room while waving a sheet of paper. His brow is covered with little beads of sweat. "Sorry for the interruption, sir. But we have just received a message from the United States!"

"If you will excuse me, I think things are starting to play out as you have said! I will return in a few moments. I would love to hear about some of the achievements both the US and Russia will have in the future! In the meantime, perhaps have some of our famous, or should I say 'infamous' vodka! Ha-ha! No. No. Just kidding! But Olaf and Yuri, you two knock yourselves out!"

Khrushchev follows his messenger and is escorted towards another exit.

"Knock yourselves out he says? Knock yourselves . . ." Yuri says, "How about I knock *him* out! Olaf, let's go!"

With a surprising amount of speed for two such bulky men, Yuri and Olaf spring to their feet and tag-team tackle the guards nearest to them.

Yuri tucks his head down and throws his arms around the waist of a guard, executing a powerful football styled tackle.

Olaf, on the other hand, does things a little differently; he waits for his targeted guard to draw his gun, and with the ease of a trained martial artist, knocks the gun from his hand and follows it up with a kick to the groin. He easily retrieves the gun from the ground while stepping on the guard's outstretched hand, in a last attempt to reclaim his weapon. By this time, Yuri has also claimed a weapon, his own weapon, the one the guard had taken from him upon our unwelcomed entrance.

Khrushchev's men push him down and out the exit. They begin to open fire on Yuri and Olaf, not minding at all that the two other guards are caught in the crossfire, or the fact that *we* could also be hit. "Chuck! The Cabinet!" I yell as I attempt to push the cabinet over for cover. It doesn't budge until Chuck and Vasily assist me. Pete shields Abby as we all take shelter behind the massive wooden cabinet. Farewell Faberge eggs!

CHAPTER TWENTY-ONE

The cabinet slams to the ground with one fell swoop. Its glass cover shatters and several decorated eggs tumble out onto the marble floor. This causes Olaf and Yuri to turn back towards us.

Both now brandishing weapons, they also seek shelter behind the cabinet, all the while returning shots to Krushev's guards.

"If we remind Khrushchev of his own kids, why isn't he stopping his guards from shooting at us?" asks Pete as he smothers Abby. She doesn't quite mind right now and I don't blame her.

Olaf continues to return fire while Yuri shouts, "Gimmee that thing!" as he snatches the temporal device from Vasily's hands. Vasily tries to maintain his hold on it but it slips from his grasp. Yuri is the victor once again.

He takes the device and knocks it over Vasily's head. Vasily loses any balance he had on the floor and begins to rub his head. He seems to be okay; he's just a little stunned and, of course, bruised. All we need is another malfunctioning and damaged time device!

"You bastard!" shouts Chuck as he lunges for Olaf. He lands a punch square across Olaf's jaw.

Olaf is unfazed. He rubs his jaw, spits some blood and aims his gun at Chuck. But in doing so, he takes a more upright posture, exposing his upper body. He quickly receives a shot to the shoulder and lets out an immense cry. One of Khrushchev's guards finally took proper aim. Now, preoccupied with his shooter, Olaf turns from Chuck and, once again, returns fire.

I've had enough. But I have no idea how to get us out of this. And then, as if a sign from God, I spot it. While hovering over Abby for protection, the back of Pete's shirt lifts up and reveals the handle of the freeze ray, tucked under his waistband. He must have picked it up after I dropped it!

I grab the handle of the freeze ray and free it from his pants. I climb over the rest of them and turn to Yuri who is nearest to me. I act fast and, making sure I don't make the same mistake as Olaf, maintain my cover. I draw the freeze ray and shout over the flying bullets, "Enough! Put down your guns! All of you!"

Vasily translates and repeats everything I say so Khrushchev's guards can also understand.

"This is a weapon from the future!" I exclaim. "It has 101 settings and is now set to freeze ray! Your weapons are inferior to this gun!"

Vasily finishes translating as Olaf drops his

weapon and holds his hands in the air. At this, and out of their curiosity, the Soviet guards stop firing. Yuri, on the other hand, is not fully convinced, but as he realizes he is the only one left in the firefight he pauses and looks interested.

"Ha! Boy, what are you talking about? Superior weapon? That looks like basic toy gun. You probably found laying around here in one of those display cases."

"Are you sure, Yuri?" asks Olaf.

"Of course! Khrushchev collects all kind of things." He says confidently.

"Give me toy, little boy. Ha-ha! I made rhyme. Give it to me now!" he says, aiming his pistol at me. Chuck and Pete catch my eye. They both nod in unison. That could only mean one thing; they are thinking what I'm thinking. I gotta act fast and I gotta act now.

In a split second I push Olaf away from me and dive to the right while firing the freeze ray at Yuri. A blast of cold and ice shoots out of the ray and solidifies around his hand and pistol. Thankfully, he never gets a shot off. He is not yet finished, though.

He stares down at his frozen gun-holding hand, looks back at me then back at his hand as the rest of us remain silent.

Yuri pulls his arm back and repeatedly slams his hand on the side of the overturned cabinet. The ice finally cracks and he breaks free from his frozen handcuff. Now that this angry bear of a man is

179

heated, I only have one choice.

I raise the freeze ray one more time and fire. Only this time, I don't let go of the trigger so quickly. I blast him with the beam of ice as it completely covers him from head to toe and begins to freeze instantaneously.

Everyone looks at me with astonished eyes. I have to admit, I am pretty surprised at myself, as well. But, it's my only option; he would have pulled that trigger, no doubt. And, as I stare at the frozen Yuri, believe it or not, it looks like he is still blinking under that huge block of ice.

"Now, put down your weapons! All of you!" orders Chuck as he points to Yuri. "Unless, that is, you want to end up looking like him!"

"Yeah! We'll turn all your asses into Yetis! Ha-ha!" Pete says while attempting a high five, which Abby does not return. She instead shakes her head in a look of pity. Pete sadly brings his hand back down to his side.

Every last Soviet soldier runs out of the room. But we still have to worry about Olaf. This proves to be easier then imagined as he quickly drops his weapon, puts his hand on his head and falls to his knees.

"Jon! The temporal! It's frozen in his back pocket!"

Sure enough, I had encapsulated our only way home in Yuri's back pocket.

"How are we gonna get it out?" asks Abby.

180

"Ha-ha! Foolish children. I knew you would foul up eventually!" says Olaf with his boorish smile.

"Shut up or I'll blast you!" says Pete as he grabs the ray from my hand and quickly aims it down at Olaf's head. He smiles and retreats in silence as he relaxes his head on the marble floor.

"Jon. What do we do?" says Abby.

"Get a chisel," laughs Pete while not taking an eye off of Olaf.

"Shut up, Pete!" scolds Abby.

"No. No, wait. He's right!" says Chuck. "It's our only way to get it, besides melting the ice in a fireplace or something."

"Yeah! Let's do that one!" says Pete, releasing one hand from the freeze ray and giving Chuck a thumbs up.

Perhaps he was right. "But with what?" I ask as we frantically look around and hope we can figure this out before the Soviet guards return with more men.

"How about this?" Vasily says as he picks up one of the elegant Faberge eggs.

"Dude, that one? Out of all of them? That one?" He happens to be holding the prized egg of the final tsar of Russia.

"It doesn't matter! We need to get out of here and fast!" claims Vasily.

"Besides," adds Abby, "once we get back, none of this will have ever happened!"

Abby, as usual, is right. Once we go back to

181

1940's Chicago, this event will be in the future and will never happen this way again.

If it works out, all will be well.

Reluctantly agreeing, I nod my head and take the egg from Vasily. I bend the top back with its golden hinge and reveal its gears inside. The gears' sharp points will work perfectly as a chisel.

I approach the frozen Russian under the watchful eye of Olaf as he looks up from the ground. I take another look at the egg and back at the solid mass of ice under which the temporal device is frozen. I scrape a little piece of ice, gently, but quickly, to test it out. It seems to be working. The ice is a lot softer than I had imagined. I'm just thankful it didn't shatter him into a million pieces like it did our model plane. I am not sure why, though? Maybe it was calibrated to have a lesser impact on humans, not to kill, but just immobilize.

I continue to carve away at the ice that covers the back pocket region of Yuri, being careful not to damage the device and, at the same time, careful not to free him too much. This crazy Russian is not a happy camper right now.

I make it to the top of the pocket as the final ice chunks fall on the floor. The egg falls, too, as I drop it and let it hit the ground. I still hate using such a rare piece as a tool. But then again, like Abby said, if all goes right, all will go back to normal.

I reach into his pocket with the few fingers that fit through the small chiseled hole, and retrieve the device. I breathe a sigh of relief as my inspection of the device reveals it is undamaged, the screen is still active and everything else seems to be as it was before.

"Ostanovis! Stop! Stop!" yells a Soviet guard entering through the other wing, heading a newly formed group of reinforced men. This just gets better and better.

CHAPTER TWENTY-TWO

We get down behind the huge cabinet once again. As I duck, I feel like I am playing the clumsy role of Pete as the device slips out of my hand. The wetness and residue of the ice made it easy for me to lose my grip. Thankfully, Abby crawls back towards the wall and retrieves it without fail.

"Hit it, Abby! Hit it!" cries Pete.

"No! Not yet! We can't do it here! Vasily says.

"What? Why not!?" questions Pete.

"Vasily's right!" I say. "We can't be this close to these goons when we activate it."

"Or else they will come back with us! Gotcha, Jon!" says Pete as he smiles a goofy smile and I nod back.

I have to think of something right now. The guards have stopped. They hold their position at what they deem to be a safe distance. Other guards now enter and block all other previously accessible exits. There aren't any windows nearby so that's out. Well, might as well use what they fear the most while we still have it.

The guards move in on us. I take one last look around and survey the room and at the last second I look up. There is a huge chandelier in the center of the room. It reminds me of the one we saw in the plantation house when Chuck was showing us around. I guess I could freeze it and make it drop. That would cause a huge commotion and give us enough time to escape. Or would it? Maybe a more drastic plan is in order.

Without wasting any more time consulting the others, who have now placed their hands on their heads as ordered by the guards, I roll the freeze ray's dial to adjust its intensity. At least . . . I think that's what it does.

Now, I'm the only one without my hands on my head. Vasily tells me the guards are directing me to do so with their commands of, "Polozhite ruki na golovu!" But instead of putting my hands on my head, I take position, raise the freeze ray and fire it at the slowly decreasing empty space between us and the guards. They back up as I get closer and continue to pull the trigger in an attempt to build an icy wall between us.

The barrier gets higher and higher and longer and longer as I connect it to the left and right walls closest to us. The commands of the guards get muted under the loud roar of the freeze ray as it builds our icy barrier.

"Quick! Everyone over there!" I yell as I put

185

the finishing touches on the wall. We run towards the ice wall and away from the two Russian trolls. We order Olaf to keep his face buried in the ground, and well, Yuri isn't going anywhere anytime soon.

Tink. Tink Tink.

"What's that noise?" asks Abby.

"It must be the ice melting!" says Pete.

Tink. Tinkity-tink. Tink.

"No! It's not melting! It's cracking! Look!" says Chuck as he points out a crack forming at the base of the wall.

"No!" Vasily says, "It's not the cracks making that sound. It's the sound making the cracks!"

"What the hell?" Pete puts into words what we are all thinking.

"The noise is bullets hitting the wall! The guards are trying to shoot us through the wall!" explains Vasily.

"What the –"

"No time, Pete!" I insist. "Quick, Abby! Hit the recall button! Hit it now and pull the trigger!" I scream, as the wall begins to shatter behind us.

"It's not . . . It's not wor–"

Silence. Thankfully, as opposed to what Abby was about to say, the device *is* working. It's working just fine. The recall journey has begun. The familiar blur of items beyond the device's reach and the other sensations that follow now encompass our senses.

Although blurry, I can see that our wall did not withstand the Russian bullets for that long. But it's no matter. At least we made it out alive and not injured at all. I hope. Only time will tell.

I can also see that Olaf has gotten up and finished chiseling Yuri out from his neck up. I am kinda glad I didn't entomb him in ice forever; the punishment he will get in a Soviet work camp will be more than any frozen death could compete with.

I start losing site of the 1961 Russian setting and begin to see signs of our last location. Then I slowly remember and realize that, since we used the recall button, we will be in the exact same spot as when we left. And if memory serves correct, the cops were approaching us. Pete remembers as well. He points at the police cars that get clearer and clearer as we finish transporting.

To the left, I see the car that we were driving before we went to Moscow. It has since crashed into a street lamp and is steaming from its busted front end.

"Jon, what do we do?" Pete asks.

The police officers, lights, sirens and all, arrive at our location. Valentina is handcuffed in the back seat of the first car. Her window is down and she screams as the squad car comes to a screeching halt.

"Look! There! I told you! I told you! They were gone for a moment and now are back! But . . . where . . . where are Olaf and Yuri? What did you do

187

to them?!" She looks at the pavement and then back at us. "Pshh! You know what? I don't even care about those jerks! Leaving me here all alone to fend for myself. Serves them right! *Whatever* you kids did to them!"

The young officer, Officer Johnson, is a bit more cautious once he realizes what she's saying may be true. He approaches us with his gun drawn.

We gain our cognizance at different times. Vasily is the last one to fully make it back. He is happy to see that it worked and that we're all back where we started from. But now he sees the current situation at hand as the officer approaches with his gun.

"Okay, guys," says Officer Johnson, "Everything is gonna be alright now. Where did those two big guys get off to?" he asks as we all exchange glances at each other, not sure of what to say.

"Um, they uh . . . um, we had to shoot them with an ice ray and-"

"Pete!" Abby cries. "Sorry, sir. He is just, well, under a lotta stress is all."

"I can understand that. Should I call a medic for you guys?" he asks as he looks over at the crashed car, not realizing that we weren't in it when it crashed. We were miles, and well, *years* away.

"You okay?"

"No. Yeah, we're fine." I say. "The guys ran down that way right after the car crashed."

"This way? Okay, thanks," he says as he

directs two police cars arriving at the scene. "Well, at least we got that 'Valentine' lady. And I'm confident those men can't be too far away."

"Thanks, officer," says Chuck.

"No. Thank you! Thank all of you for being so brave. I am not sure what just happened. But if what that crazy Russian lady was saying is true, then you guys surely just saved the world from those crazy Communists! Time travel!" he says while shaking his head and smiling, "I just can't believe it. I knew you guys were working on something in that laboratory, but . . . time travel! Guess that figures why there are so many out-of-towner scientists here recently."

"No. They were just making a huge atomic-"

"Time machine!" Abby says before Pete is able to finish. "A huge atomic time machine!" She smiles at Pete and turns her head in an air of perfection.

"Oh, yeah. That's what they've been doing. But you gotta keep it on the down-low, okay?" asks Pete.

"Down-low?"

"Yeah. Um, hush-hush. Ya know?" says Pete.

"Yeah, I get it! I like it! My lips are zipped you crazy kids!"

"You will love it in the future! We even have a black-"

"NO!" the officer pleads. "Please, I don't want to know anything about the future! I'm the type

189

of guy who believes that good things come to those who wait! I didn't even sneak a peek at any of my Christmas gifts until wakin' early Christmas morning. Ha-ha!"

"Awww! No worries, officer. I got you!" says Pete.

"Okay, guys. Well, besides the time travel stuff, which quite honestly I'm not too sure how I feel about, I need to ask you guys a few questions and to make a statement, alright? And no running off this time, ya hear!" The cop smiles.

"Well, that sounds good," I say. "But we three really need to get going. Is there any way that Chuck and Vasily can take care of that stuff? I mean, they know the whole story about the time travel and spies and stuff."

"Oh. Well. Geez," he says, taking off his patrol hat and scratching his head. "This is gonna be one helluva report!" He turns and begins to walk away. I hear him add under his breath, "One helluva report. And from me, a rookie . . . a black rookie." He stops, turns back to us and says, "Ya know, that'll be fine. In fact, I'll a . . . just give me your names and I'll fill in the rest. They kidnapped you right?"

"Yeah at gunpoint and then took us back in time and . . ."

"Okay, let's just leave that part out, guys! In fact, you two, just sign your names here and give me your dorm room numbers and we'll call it a day."

"Sounds good to us!" I say as we all share in
190

a chuckle as the cop returns to his car and Valentina.

I turn to face Chuck eye to eye and say, "Well, looks like we saved the world again, huh Chuck, old boy!"

"Ha-ha! Indeed! And we owe it all to the Brewster Boys."

"Ahummmmm," Abby says with rolled eyes.

"Oh, and Abby, of course!"

"It was nice to meet you, Vasily," I say. "Thanks for making the right decision. And trust me, it *was* the right decision." I say, putting my hand on his shoulder.

"For my sake, I hope you are right, Jon. And I hope that things go a bit better for me than you say they will."

"I hope so, too, man. I really do. You have proven you deserve it." We shake hands as Pete and Abby say their goodbyes, as well.

"Well, I guess we say goodbye, now. Again." I say to Chuck.

"Yeah, but you'll see me again in the future, right, as an old man, ha-ha."

"I don't think so. You said, well, in the future, you said that the only reason you moved into our neighborhood was to get in touch with us and tell us how to set things right. Since things are right again, I guess you have no reason to move to our neck of the woods anymore. Ya know?"

"I never thought of that, actually. Well, who knows, maybe we can stay in touch, somehow."

191

"Only time will . . ."

"Tell. I know. I know." Chuck adds.

"See ya, Chuck!" yells Pete as he gives Chuck a high five. "Great to see you again, man!"

"Same here, Pete! Don't forget, you guys still owe me a movie!"

"Ha-ha, yeah! And concessions!" adds Pete.

"That's right!" says Chuck.

"Hey, maybe Jon and I can make a trip back to the '50's or something and you can finally give us those surfing lessons!"

"Sounds good, Pete! You guys better get going. The longer you spend here the more chance there is of messing up something else in the future!"

"You're right!" I say looking at the device.

"Just make sure you don't hit the recall button this time or you will face one angry, frozen Russian!"

"True that, Chuck!" says Pete as I change the date on the temporal.

"Pete, do I have the right coordinates for the park?" I show Pete the device and he gives me a thumbs up followed with a, "Yup." I give Chuck a final fist bump goodbye and pull the trigger.

We wave goodbye through the haze and blurriness of time travel as Chuck, Vasily and the entire campus fade away. And once again, just like that, we are back in the park: no headaches, no backaches and an extremely peaceful arrival. Vasily really knew his stuff in making those changes.

"Wow, Vasily really knew his stuff, huh, Jon?"

"Ha! Yeah. I was literally just thinking the same thing."

We stand up on the lush summer grass of the park and dust ourselves off.

"I sure hope they don't make another temporal device back in the past and mess up everything again!" says Pete.

"Ummm, we took the missing blueprint pages," Abby says, holding up the pages. "So, there is no way that is gonna happen, dumb-dumb. Geez, why are you so dumb, Peter? You'd think as often as you hang out with Jon, that some of his smarts would rub off on you."

"Hey, shut up, Abby, I'm getting tired of you making fun of me all the time. And besides, I know we took the blueprints with us, but that doesn't mean that Chuck and Vasily can't create one together from memory. Or maybe Vasily made copies of the blueprints! Ever think of that? Maybe he'll have second thoughts and just decide to build another one! Who knows?!"

"I used to like you, Abby. Ya know that? But you can be a real bitch sometimes. For real! And another thing, I-"

Abby turns around, grabs Pete's shirt, pulls him toward her and plants one on his lips.

Wow! I knew it was bound to happen, eventually, but I honestly did not see that one coming. And from the look on his face, neither did Pete.

Abby pulls away from Pete and says, "As you were saying."

"Wha . . . What the hell was that? You randomly kiss me after I call you a 'B.' I don't get you, Abby. Not at all."

Talk about an awkward silence. And I thought our adventure was over.

"So . . . um, like," Pete stammers and stutters, "You wanna . . . you wanna go to homecoming with me, Abby?"

"Pete, It's July. So duuuuuuumb!"

"Fine, Abby. I didn't want to go with you anyways. I was right the first time, you're sucha-"

"Yes," says Abby.

"Yes? Yes, what?" asks Pete.

"Yes, I'll go with you to the dance."

"Oh. Okay, then. Um. Cool."

"What were you about to say? Hmmm?" asks Abby with raised eyebrows.

"He was gonna say you're sucha great soccer player. Now let's get going, you kooky lovebirds!"

CHAPTER TWENTY-THREE

I lead the way as we walk in a freaky kind of silence, with Pete and Abby, of all things, holding hands. I mean, what just happened? Crazy kids. Oh well, I hope it works out.

You know what they say about friends becoming more than friends. Well, when it's over it's over. Because, let's face it, we're teenagers and these things don't last. When it's over, it'll be kind of difficult for those two to become friends again.

Then again, knowing these two, they won't make it a week. But I won't play the role of the downer. I'll let them be. I will keep my loads of advice at bay…for now.

Besides, I have to make sure all is well in the good ol' U S of A. I sure hope we didn't mess up anything. That would suck. I dunno about those two, but I am definitely done with time travel for a while. The funny thing is, I'm pretty sure I said that last time, as well. Only one way to find out I guess. Off to the plantation house we go.

A blue pickup truck pulls alongside us.

"Hey, Jon. It's Bobby!" says Pete.

"Wuddup, guys! What are you two doing holding hands? This is crazy! This is huge! So that's why I had to cover for ya'll?

"Ha, shut up, Bobby," says Pete.

"What are you up to?" I ask.

Bobby puts his truck in park and opens the door. He heads to the truck bed which is covered with a blue tarp. He pulls it back and reveals an enormous cooler filled to the brim with fresh fish.

"Nice lookin' Micropterus salmoides," says Abby.

"I am sure that's their scientific name, Abby, but we just call them largemouth bass!" says Bobby.

"Wow! I always thought we were catching trout!" Pete says, scratching his head while Abby does her usual eye roll. Some things never change.

"Good job, man! Nice haul!" I say.

"Yeah. Next week I'm flying out to go fishing in Lake Tahoe! Should be awesome!"

"Wait, what? Lake Tahoe? In Nevada?"

"Come on, Jon. You know my uncle has a place in Tahoe! I'm finally getting a chance to go fishing out there."

"I know! I know! But like, nothing funny out that way, huh?"

"Funny? You feeling alright, dude? Whadaya mean?"

"Yeah, funny. Like alien invasion or massive earthquakes or, a . . . I dunno, a Communist takeover?"

196

"Ha, you guys and your comic books, I swear! None of that in Tahoe, man. Aliens are over in Area 51! You know that!"

We all share a laugh.

"Nothing strange in Tahoe except those giant goldfish that someone dumped. Shoot I'd be happy with catching one of those, though. I don't care!"

"That's great news! Great news, Bobby!" I say as I give him a thumbs up.

"Ha, thanks man. But it's not too great. Those giant fish are really messing with the other fish in the lake and they say-."

"No, no, Bobby," interrupts Pete, "Jon is right. That really is great news!"

"Yeah, man. You guys should come sometime. Not this time, though, 'cuz we already got our plane tickets, so . . ."

"Sounds great, Bobby. I would love to see all the nifty fifty United States one day."

I purposefully say that to ask him how many states there are without really asking him at all. But he hasn't answered yet and has a weird expression on his face. Dear God, please tell me there are still fifty states and everything is back to normal.

"Um . . . ya know, Bobby? To see all, um, fifty states?" I say while holding my breath. Abby and Pete are less focused on each other now and also await Bobby's response. It's as if time has slowed down. Come on, Bobby, out with it!

"Yeah, man of course that would be great. Just don't know why you called them, nifty."

"Oh! Ha-ha! Is that all? It's a song, buddy. Just an old song." We breathe another, all too familiar, sigh of relief.

"Cool. Well, yeah, next year then. Just remind me and we can all go!"

"Sounds good," I reply.

"Okay, well, I gotta get back to helpin' out my dad. He just won another storage unit auction and I gotta help him haul the treasures!" he says as he gets back into his truck and drives away.

"See ya, Bobby!" we all say in tandem.

"Good news, huh, Jonny boy?" says Pete.

"Yeah, most def! Well, at least there are fifty states again. There is only one true way to find out if everything is straight; we need to get my history textbook."

"Onward to the treehouse!!!" Pete screams at the top of his lungs, while Abby, instead of rolling her eyes, gives him a smile of acceptance.

We continue our walk to the treehouse as we take in the familiar sites of our neighborhood and its surroundings, ever vigilante of the slightest discrepancy. So far so good.

Another familiar vehicle passes us and honks its horn. It's Mr. Lee and his wife. They must be coming home from the nursery since their trunk is half open with a little tree sticking out. One more familiar clue that things are back to normal.

We round the corner and make our way to my street. There it is, our home away from home, our refuge, our treehouse. I throw open the gate and run towards the rope ladder.

"Hey, Jon, tuck in the freeze ray," says Abby as she follows me up the rope. "That thing saved us once already and who knows, it may save us again one day!"

I reach around my back pocket, push the freeze ray deeper and continue my climb into the treehouse. I push open the main hatch and climb in. Everything here looks in place, or, that is to say, out of place. But that's normal. Maybe sometime this summer I'll get a chance to clean this mess.

There it is, my American history textbook, right where I left it. I quickly reach for it and turn to the map section while Abby and Pete make their way into the treehouse.

"What's it say, Jon? What's it say?" asks Pete as he closes the entrance hatch. I quickly thumb through the pages. It takes an eternity just to reach the map section, but there it is! America, the US of A, in all its unified, undivided glory. Thank God!

"It's fine, guys! It's fine! All fifty are here and all fifty are ours!" I say as I hold open the two pages that display the map of the United States.

"Yes!" Jon says as we all go up for a group high five.

Bzzzz. Bzzzz. My phone vibrates alerting me that I have a new message waiting on one of my many social networking sites. At the same time, Pete's phone rings a tone and Abby's says, "tweet, tweet."

"Whoa, what are the odds?" says Pete.

"I know right. Who could it be?" asks Abby as she fumbles with her smiley-face novelty phone case.

I can only think of one person who would contact us all at the same time.

"Dude, it's Chuck!" Pete says as he zooms in and expands his fingers on his phone. "He says, 'Hey you guys. Been a while. Well, many years for me but only a few hours or so for you I guess. I have waited a long time to contact you guys since Chicago and, well, here we are. I moved back to Hawaii in the 1980's and am loving retirement. Thanks for saving the day once again. I am sure you have noticed everything is back to normal . . . except one thing.'"

"Except one thing!" Abby cries.

Pete replies, "Son of a-"

"Keep reading, Pete!" I say

"Okay! Right! Where was I? . . . 'Except one thing. Are you ready for it, because this one is big. I mean it. If you guys thought Pearl Harbor and Soviet Russia were big you won't believe this one. Please take a seat while reading this . . .'"

We heed Chuck's advice and take a seat before Pete continues reading.

"'Just kidding! Everything is fine!! Got you guys!' Oh, man!"

"Got 'em!" says Abby.

"Yeah, he sure did. He got all of us!" Pete comments as he continues to read.

"'Sorry! I had to get you guys one last time. I would love to have you all visit me sometime in Hawaii. As you know, I am getting old and, well. It would be nice to see you again. At least we can webcam sometime if I ever figure this thing out! Don't forget to add me and follow me!' Good old tech savvy, Chuck. Well, at least we know everything is okay." Pete says as he puts his phone away.

"Yup, that is until our next adventure comes around, Pete." I say. "Although, I think you two are about to embark on your own little summer adventure! Ha-ha!"

"Shut up, Jon!" says Abby.

"Uh-oh! Now you're telling *me* to shut up. Ya gonna kiss *me* next?"

"In your dreams, Jon!"

"So, now that this adventure is over, when we gonna try out the other gadgets in the bag, Jon?" Pete asks in an obvious attempt to change the subject.

"No time soon. Can't be too safe with these things. And, I think we need to put the freeze ray and the temporal back in the safe deposit box with the others. Shoot, we do need a break, though, for real. We should have asked Vasily and Chuck if all this time traveling will cause any health issues for us, ya know?"

"Righto! Good thinking, old chap! Pip, Pip,

201

Cheerio!" Pete says in his cockney accent.

"I can't wait to ask my mom about her family now that California is American again." I say.

"Yeah," says Pete. "That was sooooome adventure. We should call ourselves the 'Adventure Club' or something!"

"Lame!" says Abby.

"Whatever!" says Pete as he kicks Abby's right shoe.

Not wanting to be in another moment of awkward silence, I say, "So what was Olaf and Yuri's problem anyway?"

"I know, right! And, Jon! Sooooo ballsy of you to shoot Yuri with the freeze ray! I didn't think you had it in you, man!" Pete admits.

"You kiddin' me? I'd do anything to protect you two. Besides, like Chuck said, we're the Brewster Boys! Ha-ha."

"Uhummm."

"And Abby! And Abby!" Pete adds while pushing Abby's shoulder with his.

We sit on the bean bags and share a laugh, finishing this, our second adventure in one week: remembering, reflecting and reminiscing. Who knows what the future holds? As they say, only time will tell. All I know is, I hope we don't find out anytime soon!

THE END

ABOUT THE AUTHOR

The Brewster Boys and the Red Revenge is the second in a series of books by Stephen J. Dittmer. Stephen graduated from George Mason University with a Bachelor's in History and a Master's in Education. He currently teaches high school social studies in Prince William County, Virginia.

Keep updated with news and new releases!

"Like" the Brewster Boys on Facebook

www.facebook.com/TheBrewsterBoysAndTheEveOf Infamy

BOOK ONE –
> *The Brewster Boys and the Eve of Infamy*

BOOK TWO –
> *The Brewster Boys and the Red Revenge*

BOOK THREE –
> **TBA**

Made in the USA
Charleston, SC
20 July 2016